Cover Design and Interior format by The Killion Group
http://thekilliongroupinc.com

HIGHLAND HIGHLIGHTS

THE BEST OF LOKI GRANT

KEIRA MONTCLAIR

FOREWORD

WELCOME TO THE Highlights Series!

Yes, you have read most of these scenes! Most books will have new, exclusive scenes that have only been seen by a few but please know you, my faithful fans, have ALREADY READ most of these scenes in my previous books. You don't want to pay for them again? Then please don't. Wait until they are all out and sign up for Kindle Unlimited. Then you can read them for free.

Now a little bit about this series.

The inspiration for the series came from the fact that I have fifty-five books in the combined Grant/Ramsay series, and even I can no longer remember everything. I have so many different notebooks, software notes, journals, and story bibles that tracking down any one bit of information had become a true labor.

The first issue? I couldn't recall the ages and hair colors of all the bairns. There are simply too many of them. I often wished I had a book with just the bairns listed so I could easily retrieve their ages and characteristics.

Then along came the faeries, the swords, the angels, and the seers. Who had what power? I lost track.

So I decided to go through all fifty-five books and copy and paste the relevant scenes into a reference file. My next thought? Wouldn't my readers love it if I did the same thing with Alex Grant and Logan Ramsay? Would they buy a book like that?

I'm hoping you'll say yes!

The project grew from there. As of this writing, I have plans for the following highlights books, to be titled *The Best of*:

Alexander Grant
Madeline Grant
Logan Ramsay
Gwyneth Ramsay
Loki Grant
Brenna Ramsay
Torrian Ramsay
Connor Grant
Maitland Menzie
Dyna Grant
The Bairns, Part 1 and 2
The Pets, Ghosts, and Spirits
My Favorite Scenes

That's right. It quickly went from four books to thirteen, and a few of them have too many favorite scenes to fit in one volume. Logan wins for the longest, but he would tell you that was only right.

I may not have chosen your favorite, but each collection had to be long enough to reach novella size. You loved Drew, Quade, or Aedan more? Not enough for a book. There are other possibilities, if you my beloved readers ask for them. The best of the weddings, the Camerons, the villains? Maybe someday in the future, but it will be a while, because this was a long, tedious project. Long. Did I say long? It took me forever!

I tried to stick to a few rules:

There is no set order to read the series. You can read in any order. I also will have a random release schedule, not necessarily in the order listed above.

I tried to take only three or four scenes from the character's main book. I took the scenes that most represented his or her personality or an important stage in their life.

Excerpts are presented *exactly* as they appeared in each book. All those comma errors? I didn't change them. Other than a few glaring typos, nothing was changed.

I did my best to orient the reader to each scene by adding a line or two before each excerpt. Chapters are listed with the title of each book so you can reference them if you like.

The series and books are ordered chronologically. In other words, Highland Healers comes before Highland Swords, which is *not* how I released them.

Did I miss your favorite scene? Probably. Understand that I had thirteen tabs open on my laptop as I slowly perused each book.

I will also add a trigger warning here as a reminder that Medieval times were brutal.

Are you ready for *The Best of Loki Grant*, the wee lad who stole everyone's heart? Then read on.

My thoughts will be written in italics before the beginning of each scene.

Let me know what you think!

Keira Montclair

CONTENT WARNING:

The world in which my beloved Grants and Ramsays live is violent in many ways. You will read about the horrors of war, sexual assault, traumatic births, child abuse, and other events we find shocking today. Please be aware of your reactions as you read and step away if you need to.

NOVELS BY
KEIRA MONTCLAIR

Clan Grant/Clan Ramsay World

<u>THE CLAN GRANT SERIES</u>

#1- RESCUED BY A HIGHLANDER-
Alex and Maddie
#2- HEALING A HIGHLANDER'S HEART-
Brenna and Quade
#3- LOVE LETTERS FROM LARGS-
Brodie and Celestina
#4-JOURNEY TO THE HIGHLANDS-
Robbie and Caralyn
#5-HIGHLAND SPARKS-
Logan and Gwyneth
#6-MY DESPERATE HIGHLANDER-
Micheil and Diana
#7-THE BRIGHTEST STAR IN THE HIGHLANDS-
Jennie and Aedan
#8- HIGHLAND HARMONY-
Avelina and Drew
#9-YULETIDE ANGELS

<u>THE HIGHLAND CLAN</u>

LOKI-Book One
TORRIAN-Book Two
LILY-Book Three

JAKE-Book Four
ASHLYN-Book Five
MOLLY-Book Six
JAMIE AND GRACIE-Book Seven
SORCHA-Book Eight
KYLA-Book Nine
BETHIA-Book Ten
LOKI'S CHRISTMAS STORY-Book Eleven
ELIZABETH-Book Twelve

THE BAND OF COUSINS

HIGHLAND VENGEANCE
HIGHLAND ABDUCTION
HIGHLAND RETRIBUTION
HIGHLAND LIES
HIGHLAND FORTITUDE
HIGHLAND RESILIENCE
HIGHLAND DEVOTION
HIGHLAND BRAWN
HIGHLAND YULETIDE MAGIC

HIGHLAND HEALERS

THE CURSE OF BLACK ISLE
THE WITCH OF BLACK ISLE
THE SCOURGE OF BLACK ISLE
THE GHOSTS OF BLACK ISLE
THE GIFT OF BLACK ISLE

HIGHLAND SWORDS

THE SCOT'S BETRAYAL
THE SCOT'S SPY
THE SCOT'S PURSUIT
THE SCOT'S QUEST

THE SCOT'S DECEPTION
THE SCOT'S ANGEL

HIGHLAND HUNTERS
THE SCOT'S CONFLICT
THE SCOT'S TRAITOR
THE SCOT'S PROTECTOR
THE SCOT'S VOW
THE SCOT'S DESTINY
THE SCOT'S WARNING
THE SCOT'S RECKONING
THE SCOT'S LEGACY

CLANS OF MULL
THE PLIGHT OF A SCOTTISH LASS
THE BURDEN OF A SCOTTISH CHIEFTAIN
THE ANGUISH OF THE SCOTTISH LAIRDS
THE TORMENT OF A SCOTTISH WARRIOR
THE DEFIANCE OF A SCOTTISH HEART
THE WRATH OF A SCOTTISH BLADE

CLAN GRANT
1260

LOVE LETTERS FROM LARGS

Book 3

BRODIE AND CELESTINA

Loki became a favorite from this first book. I'm not sure exactly why. Was it Missy Angel? The way Alex accepted him into the clan? I think it was most likely his cheekiness, and this first scene is a great illustration of the boy's character.

CHAPTER TWELVE

Brodie is at a loss because he cannot find Celestina. Who knew help would come in the form of a wee ruffian who lived behind an inn in Ayr? And yes, the lad was indeed spying…

BRODIE AND NICOL stood in the middle of town, Nicol paying close attention to their surroundings while his friend picked up every twig and stick in the area to shred and toss at will.

"I swear if you do no' stop your pacing, everyone will know your intent," Nicol smiled.

Brodie stopped for long enough to glare at his friend. "I swear if you do no' wipe that incessant grin off your face, I'll do it for you."

"What do you want to do next? Ivarsson is a rich man, and 'tis said he has several homes. No one knows where he took her." Nicol stared up and down the road, as if willing the passersby to give them information.

"Somebody has to know something," Brodie barked. "I can no' believe the most beautiful lass in all of Ayrshire was moved out of the village without anyone noticing." He reached for more sticks to tear apart but found none. Circling a copse of trees for more, he ran right into a young lad who had been standing sentinel just around the corner.

"Lad, watch where you are about. You can no' just walk into people," Brodie roared as he helped the boy up and set him aside.

"I dinna run into you, master. You ran into me."

The lad's cheekiness put a smile on his face. He had to be between six and eight summers, yet he stood there as if he owned half the land. He glared at Brodie with his hands on his hips in a challenge.

Brodie wrapped his arm around the boy's waist and flipped him sideways, carrying him around the corner to Nicol. The lad's arms and legs flailed like windmills until Brodie dropped him to the ground. "Look what I found hiding in the trees behind us, Nicol. An eavesdropper."

"I wasnae spying." The boy's chin jutted up a few inches as he scuffled to his feet.

"Aye, you were, lad. I caught you." Brodie tried to hide his grin, but he couldn't. Feisty boys always reminded him of his own boyhood.

The lad crossed his arms and scrunched his face as he stared at his captor. "I was about to come out. I was just waiting."

"Waiting for what?" Brodie's eyebrow arched in anticipation.

"Waiting for you to be ready to pay me a big coin for my information. You have to wait till just the right time to get people to part with some gold, you see."

Brodie glanced at Nicol to gauge his reaction to the young sprite. His friend's eyes sparkled with amusement.

"And what information do you have worthy of a reward?" Brodie waited. This surely would prove to be entertaining. If the lad was as cheeky as he appeared, perhaps he could use him to help them find the traitors. A multitude of possibilities churned in his mind.

"I know about the angel."

A fist hit Brodie square in the gut. The angel? *His* angel? He reached over and lifted the lad off the ground until his face sat a mere inch away from his.

"What angel? Out with it, lad, if you value your tongue."

Nicol grabbed his arm. "Easy, Grant. I am sure the lad will be agreeable. Set him down and let's find out." He winked at Brodie. "And if he's not, we can leave him up in that tree for awhile."

Though he set the squirming lad down between them, Brodie kept one hand on him. He couldn't risk losing him if he chose to bolt. "What's your name?"

The boy tugged at Brodie's hand, but to no avail. "Leave me be and I'll tell you."

"I do no' think so. You'll tell me now," Brodie bellowed.

"Och, let go! Train me to be a Grant warrior like you and I'll tell you everything I know."

Squeezing his arm a bit more, Brodie said, "Your name first, then we'll negotiate."

"Och, ease off! Loki, my name is Loki."

Brodie relaxed his grip but didn't free him completely. He didn't trust the wee ruffian one bit.

"All right, Loki," he said. "What angel? If 'tis her we are looking for, I'll consider training you."

"The angel of Ayrshire. Everyone knows her. She has the long golden hair. Her father kept her locked up in the tower home at the end of that road. We could see her in the tower every once in a while. I used to watch her there. The sad angel."

"And you know where she is now?"

"Certes, I know everythin' in this town. I saw the mean bastard force her into a big cart, 'twas the biggest I ever saw."

"You have a raw mouth for a young lad. And even if what you say is true, it still does no' mean you know where the cart went."

"Ha! I noticed your moon face whenever she was around, so I decided to follow her."

Nicol's abrupt bark of laughter caught Brodie off guard. His moon face? "Do no' lie to me, lad. You followed her to steal from the man."

"Och, that, too." His lips pursed. "But you are easy to read. You'll follow her anywhere. If yer wondering how I did it, I climbed under the cart into the box and rode along. "Twas one of those fine carts, it was, with a separate compartment underneath. Aye, I do know where she is, but it'll cost you, master warrior. I knew you'd be looking for her. You must promise to train me."

Nicol's hoot echoed in the trees. This lad had bollocks the size of a bull's; Brodie had to give him that. A wise one for his age. Perhaps he could indeed be of use to them.

"All right. Where are your mother and father? I need to talk to them before I can make you a page to me."

"I got none. I dinna need a mither or a father."

"Where are they, Loki? Warriors do no' lie." Brodie gave him a little shake of encouragement.

"I am nae lying. Me mama died birthing me. I ne'er knew me da."

The lad quieted and stared at the ground after this admission. Brodie heard a loud rumbling from his belly. "Where do you live?"

"Over there," his dirty finger pointed behind a nearby inn. "I have a wooden crate in the back to hide under in the rain. Suits me fine. I can take care of meself. But I want to be a Grant warrior, like I said. 'Tis said they are the biggest and best warriors of all the Scots. I saw you come in the other day to the royal castle. And I saw the biggest laird in all the land—your laird, Alexander Grant. I want to be like you and The Grant. I promise to work hard."

Brodie sighed. The lad lived on the street and was starving. "Nicol, go get the lad a meat pie and bring it back." He handed his friend a coin before returning his attention to the sprite. "Will you promise to stay put if I feed you? Here, I have an oatcake for you till Nicol returns with the pie."

The boy nodded emphatically. He could almost see the drool about to roll down Loki's chin. He took him by the scruff of the neck and sat him down under a nearby oak tree. Hellfire, did the lad have to pull on his heartstrings so? And since when did he have any heartstrings? Heartstrings were only in lasses…or at least that's what he'd thought before meeting Celestina.

Loki grabbed the oatcake, muttered his thanks and stuffed his face in a flash. Brodie thought of his two nephews, Alex's lads. What if they had to go hungry?

Nicol returned with the meat pie and a sweet pastry. Brodie rolled his eyes at his friend. Apparently, he wasn't the only one with the failing of heartstrings.

Once the lad was happily snacking on his bounty, Brodie and Nicol sat in the grass next to him. "All right, lad. We'll train you, but you have to tell us everything you know about the angel as soon as you finish the meat pie." They waited patiently as the boy devoured his food, smacking his lips in satisfaction every once in a while. He was about to eat the sweet roll when Brodie grabbed it.

"Och, no' yet. Information first. Where did the man take the angel?"

The lad stared at the pastry with a longing that forced Brodie to look away. "Hellfire," he mumbled out of the corner of his mouth.

"He took her north. There's an old keep called Creggan Hall with a tower directly north of here. 'Tis about a day's travel on a horse near Largs. He locked her in the tower."

"Locked her up, why?"

Loki held his hand out for the pastry. The lad had timing; he had to give him that. He handed the treat over.

The lad licked the icing off the top before he spoke. "Aye, he locked her up, and he says he will no' let her go until he knows she does no' carry a babe."

"How in hell did you find that out?" Brodie glanced at Nicol. Could it be true? It made sense. The plan must have been planted in Ivarsson's head by Father Padraig. He would sleep better at night if he didn't have to think of his wife with that man's hands all over her. Perfect. The more he thought about the arrangement, the more he liked it. She'd be safe for at least a fortnight, which would give him plenty of time to kidnap her.

"I knocked on the back door and the cook gave me scraps to eat. I heard the kitchen lasses gossiping about it."

An idea popped into Brodie's head. He grinned at Nicol before he spoke. "Aye, lad, here's the plan. You have to prove to me you are a hard worker and smart, too. Can you find your way back to the tower if Nicol brings you on his horse?"

"Aye."

"Then here is your test. I have something you need to bring to the lass. Then you have to return with the proof that she received it." He nodded as he talked, suddenly excited at this new prospect. "If you are successful, we will commence your training."

"Aye, master. I'll do it." Loki pointed to Nicol. "You heard him promise me."

"Lad, I am a Grant. I do no' go back on my word. My name is Brodie, no' master. And this is Nicol."

"Aye, Master Brodie, tell me what to do. And you have to feed me, too." Loki grinned at him. "Do no' worry…they dinna call me Lucky Loki for naught."

Chapter Thirteen

Celestina is locked up in a tower and surely did not expect to see a lad climb up the garderobe, endearing as he was.

Then, all at once, a wee face popped up through the opening and a small urchin landed directly in front of her.

She waited in shock as the boy held his finger to his lips to shush her. While a snake or a bat might elicit a scream, this small child wouldn't. He was the cutest she had seen in quite some time, though she hadn't met many children to whom she could compare him.

She backed up to the table, never taking her eyes off the wee lad. When she reached her chair, she rotated it until she sat facing him. After a moment, the boy strolled over to her and whispered, "Good morn to you, Angel. My name is Lucky Loki. Master sent me, rather, Master Brodie." He giggled and then shushed himself. "We must be quiet. If I get caught, Master will no' make me a Grant warrior."

Ignoring the odor that filled the room from the wee one, Celestina swallowed and smiled at the lad. "Brodie? You know my husband, Brodie Grant?"

"Aye, he sent me. Look what I have for you."

The urchin stood close to her and promptly lifted up his shirt. A note with her name on it was at the front of a pile of blank papers tied to his belly. "These are for you, missy angel. Take them off." He jutted his wee belly at her, his shirt raised up over his head to give her access.

Her hands trembled as she untied the string, but she managed to catch the papers and set them on the table before they fell. The boy pulled his shirt down and handed her a writing utensil. "Master Brodie says I have to wait for your answer. He says you can write. Can you, missy angel?"

"Aye." She grabbed the utensil, still stunned by the sight of the lad standing in the middle of her tower prison. "How did you get here? Where did you come from? What is your name again?"

He giggled and, without any preliminaries, plopped himself on the bed. "My name is Loki. Master Brodie sent me with this note. If I bring him one back from you, he and Master Nicol will train me to be a Grant warrior. He promised."

"But how did you get in here?"

"Och, 'twas easy, missy angel. I climbed up the rungs in the garderobe."

Celestina wrinkled her nose at the raw odor emanating from the young one. "There are steps inside the garderobe?"

"Och, aye, you can sneak out in case of an attack. Course, you can no' because you are too big for the wee hole. I tried to move the piece of wood, but 'tis nailed shut. But I can sneak up. See?" He giggled and leaned back against the pillow. "I'll just rest my eyes a bit while you read and write, if you dinna mind. Wake me when you are ready, and I will take your letter back to Master Brodie. He keeps me verra busy, you see." He closed his eyes and settled back.

Celestina smiled at the lad on her bed. He was by far the dearest thing she had ever had this close to her. Children were rarely seen in her world, and he was definitely the most wonderful thing that had happened to her since her imprisonment. She reached for the note on the table, and her hand stilled, almost afraid to open it. Had Brodie changed his mind about her now that the wedding to Ivarsson had actually taken place? She closed her eyes, saying a swift prayer that he still loved her and would help her escape this prison.

As if sensing her troubled thoughts, Loki's eyes opened. "Tis all right. He is verra sweet on you, missy angel." He nodded his head in assertion and closed his eyes again.

Chapter Sixteen

Brodie loses Celestina again, but he knows who can help him find her. Lucky Loki demonstrates just how clever he is.

Loki backed away as if he was preparing to bolt. "And you also said Highlanders were to do the honorable thing and protect the weak."

Brodie held his hand up to stop Nicol's next words. His voice dropped to a whisper, understanding dawning in his gut. "Aye, we did, Loki. Tell us what you have been about."

"I have been protecting someone who can't protect herself."

"Who, Loki?" Hope sprang in Brodie's gut. Would the lad pull through for him again?

"Missy angel." He pointed to Brodie. "Ivarsson would kill you if he saw you. But I can follow her."

"Is that what you were doing? Were you outside the tower when they left? Do you know where she is?" Brodie had to force himself to cease pummeling the lad with questions.

"Aye and aye!" Loki broke out in a wide grin and nodded his head, clearly quite proud of himself. Brodie wanted to kiss the boy, but he held back since the wee lad had asked him to train him as a warrior.

Nicol, clearly stunned, asked, "How did you know they were leaving?"

"'Twas easy. I put a bunch of stones in Aldrik's shoes. I knew he would holler and bellow loud when he put his shoes on and stepped on the stones." Loki had an evil look in his eye when he said, "I put quite a few inside. They had to hurt." He threw his head back and giggled.

Nicol stared at him. "What? Speak up, lad, and stop talking in circles."

"I was afraid I would fall asleep when I was watching over my—I mean—missy angel. I wanted to know if they were leaving. If the nasty draugr left, I could sneak up and see if she was all right. So I put little rocks in the shoes of Aldrik—the draugr—so he would bellow loud enough to wake me when he put them on. He can no' leave without putting his shoes on, now, can he?"

Brodie and Nicol both grinned and nodded their heads simultaneously. "Well played, lad. Out with it."

"So when he bellowed—and they hurt him bad," he put his hand over his mouth in an attempt to contain his glee. "Sorry, so when he hollered, it woke me in the bushes and I knew they were leaving with missy angel. So I was right there when they put her in the cart with her maid and left. I did no' know she would be leaving. 'Twas a good thing I was there, Master Brodie. But Ivarsson did no' go with them."

Brodie crouched down in front of the lad and rested his arms on his legs. "Lad, tell me you know where she is, and I will buy you the biggest pastry in the land."

Loki nodded his head before he rubbed his wee belly. "And a meat pie, too? It was hard work following that caravan until I figured out where they were headed."

"Aye, two meat pies, you wee trickster. Where is she?"

"At her father's house in Lennox near Loch Lomond. I heard the guards talking about it. And Ivarsson is still here in Ayr."

Brodie picked Loki up and swung him up on his shoulders as they headed over to the local baker in the middle of town. "Well done, lad. You make me proud to call you a Grant warrior. Now, where are those meat pies?"

Chapter Twenty

I always wanted to write a scene where the heroine is saved by her hero on horseback. I just had to figure out exactly how to do it so it sounded plausible. In this scene, Celestina and Loki are waiting for Brodie, but while they wait, they meet the Norsemen near Loch Lomond, and the true value of a sling is learned.

Celestina and Loki ran and ran until she thought her lungs would burst. Much as she'd hated to leave her true husband's side, she hadn't wanted to risk all their lives by insisting otherwise. They were still in the trees, but she could tell they were drawing closer to the village because they could hear people yelling and screaming.

"Loki, promise me you will not do anything

foolish. When Brodie gets here, he will help us. We just need to find a place to hide until that happens."

Loki's chest puffed out. "Lass, I am a Grant warrior now. I will protect you with this. See?" He held up his slinger and held open his pocket, which was filled with stones of various sizes. "I am verra good with my sling. I will protect you. That is what Highlanders do."

Celestina couldn't help but smile at the lad's seriousness. They finally found a group of bushes behind a building and hid while they waited to see what was happening around them.

"Loki." She brushed some dirt off the lad's face.

"'Tis all right, missy angel. 'Tis just a wee bit of dirt. Do not bother yourself with it."

"When this is all over, you will stay with Brodie and me, will you not?"

"Och, I will be training with the Grant warriors. They promised."

"I am sure they need you, but when you have days off, you will come and live with us in the Highlands. Agreed?" She stared at the plucky, cheeky lad of whom she'd grown so fond. She did not want to lose him.

"I suppose if you insist." He stared at the stones in his pocket. "You are no' going to make me take baths, are you?"

She chuckled. "Nay, you can swim in the loch with the warriors."

He seemed to accept that, so she continued, "You will never have to go back and live in a place where you will get hit with fists."

Loki's gaze jerked back to hers. "How did you know, missy?"

"I knew because I lived in a place like that, too. I love you like a son, and I want you near me, so there will be no arguments."

Loki rolled his eyes. "All right. I know you need someone to hug." He reached over and put his finger to her lips. "Shush. Listen."

A group of drunken men argued not far from them.

"Loki, do you remember where you were when you last saw Inga?"

"Aye, but hush," he put his finger up to his lips. "I do no' want us to be discovered.You wait here while I check to see where those men are."

Celestina hid in the bushes while Loki crept out. He picked out a stone, placed it carefully in his slinger, and let it fly. A few seconds later, a man yelled out a torrent of curses she did not understand.

Loki ran back to Celestina with a grin on his face. "Got him, missy." He covered his mouth and giggled.

"Loki, be careful. He is no' English or Scottish. Whoever you hit must be Norwegian," she whispered. "He'll kill you if he catches you."

"Och, missy angel. My job is to find Nicol or, if I can no' do that, hide you until Master Brodie comes. I am just following my orders."

The lad snuck out of the trees again and came back a few moments later. "There are only three that I can see, but they look mean. I'll take care of them, missy."

Loki ran back out, and she whispered softly, "Be careful. I do no' want anything to happen to you."

He rushed back to her side with a sly grin on his face and patted her arm. "Och, I ken you love me. 'Tis all right." With that, he disappeared again until another string of curses rang out in the air. He tore back to their hiding spot in gleeful delight, clearly quite proud of his accomplishments.

"Have you seen any signs of Nicol at all, Loki?"

"Nay, those big lads are in my way. They just keep pacing the path with their great big packs over their shoulders as if they are waiting for someone. I'll get rid of them."

Twice more he ran out and peppered them with stones, before returning to their hiding place.

Then one of the men discovered their hidden spot and charged toward them with a finger pointing.

Celestina shrieked, grabbed Loki, and they turned and ran around the back of the building back through the trees. Celestina started to head into the forest, but Loki turned toward the well beaten path in the middle of the village. "Nay, Loki! This way, not the lane."

He ignored her, so she followed behind him, racing as fast as she could with her skirts swirling around her legs. She could let nothing happen to him. She broke through the trees in time to see wee Loki tearing down the middle of the path with two big warriors chasing him. She noticed one lying on the ground asleep. Had Loki actually managed to knock one of them out?

Chugging after them, she started to think Loki was going to get away when the front runner finally picked up speed and grabbed the wee lad by the arm and plucked him up off the ground, hanging him upside down for his friend to see. He beat the boy's bottom five times, and then his friend grabbed Loki and dumped him in a nearby water bucket head first while keeping a hold on his ankle.

Something snapped inside her. Without making a sound, Celestina ran into the trees and found the largest piece of wood she could find. She came out swinging and clubbed one man in the back of the head so hard he tumbled to the ground, clearly in a dead faint. The other one still held Loki with one arm, so she strolled up, swung her club, and hit him square in the chest with an angry scream. She could tell she'd stunned him, but he retained his grasp on Loki. He reached for her, but she managed to dance out of the way.

"Let him go, you big oaf. Leave him be!" Her voice reached a fevered pitch, her anger building from years of mistreatment, hours of pain, and mountains of shame.

Loki, who'd pulled his head out of the water, managed to draw out a few more stones from his pocket, which miraculously hadn't tumbled out when he'd been turned upside down, and slung them at the brute.

"You have no right! No right. You churlish bastard!" she shouted, continuing to swing her weapon. "Leave him alone." She dodged his grasp without difficulty, mostly because his movements had slowed, both from drink and the combined attack of her and Loki. He staggered in her direction, but she did not, could not stop. When he saw her arms swing high above her head, he dropped Loki and the boy sprinted away. Grinning stupidly, the man tried to grab her, but she managed to elude him again. He almost fell, but then righted himself and turned around with a dazed expression, reaching for her. She took the club and hit him as hard as she could.

His dazed expression turned dark and angry. The viciousness of his growl would have normally caused Celestina to back down, but not today. The man tried to walk toward her again. In her own mind, she knew she had lost control, but somehow she felt justice was being served.

Stalking toward him with a vengeance and a purpose previously unknown to her, she hollered at him. "No right, you have no right. Do you hear me? How dare you pick on someone smaller than you?" Visions of Loki hanging in the air fueled her anger. Tears ran down her face and she continued to swing. "You are three times his size and you pick on him. Leave him alone."

Another couple of blows, and he fell to a sitting position. Still, he continued to stare at her. Anger bubbled from within her. "Who gave you permission to touch me?" She held the club in front of her, gasping for air now. She needed to replenish her energy because she was not done. Her arms lifted again, heavy with retribution for this unknown assailant, this man who now represented all the atrocities she had ever been forced to endure. "Leave *me* alone." She swung again, and the man toppled face first into the dirt.

Powerless to stop, yet empowered with a freedom

she had never before known, she continued. Her arms reached as high as possible and she hit him again. "*Leave.*" She heaved again. "*Me.*" She bellowed with her last swing. "*Alone!*"

Her tears turned to sobs when she realized the man no longer moved. She whirled around, searching for Loki, but didn't see him anywhere. She started down the road, tears blurring her vision. Another group of bellowing Norsemen was running directly toward her. She ran back and picked up her piece of wood, now drenched in blood.

She charged down the middle of the road with her club over her head and screamed, "Nay!"

Chapter Twenty-One

Brodie had caught up with Nicol and Inga just outside of the village and made arrangements for their travel. They agreed to stay together until they found Loki and Celestina. He came down the path in time to see his wee wife running in the opposite direction with a club held over her head, straight at a group of Norsemen. Loki was running to join her, and Nicol and Inga were on horseback headed straight for Loki. As he watched, his friend swooped down to pick up the wee lad.

"Celestina!" he screamed his wife's name as loud as he could. He had to get to her before that group of warriors did.

"Celestina!" he yelled again and she finally glanced over her shoulder. The crazed look in her eyes told him he needed to get to her and fast. He galloped toward her with full force and yelled, "Arms up!"

She slowed and turned her head sideways but kept running forward. She had almost reached the Norsemen now.

"Celestina, arms up, remember my story about my sisters? Arms up! Face me!"

The warriors started to whoop in excitement.

She turned toward him and held her arms up, still running, a haunted look in her gaze.

"Drop the club, love," he shouted.

She threw the club behind her just before he leaned down to grab her around the waist, and plucked her off the ground. "Arms around my shoulders. Hang on to me."

She grabbed onto him, fighting to hang on. He struggled to right her and she floundered. "I have you, trust me." She relaxed and he settled her in front of him right before he rode past the group of warriors.

"Loki! Where is Loki?" she yelled.

"He's fine." Brodie pointed to Nicol who was not far behind them.

Celestina turned to make sure Loki was safe and promptly collapsed in sobs against her husband. She held a death grip on his tunic, and he whispered calming words in her ear. He held her as she cried and cried until she had no tears left inside.

Chapter Twenty-Six

Loki goes after Celestina to tell her about Brodie's injury.

Celestina, still inconsolable, paced in the great hall. She had just returned from her riding lessons with her father. Learning to ride a horse well had been difficult work, but she was proud of her accomplishments, and she knew it was a skill she needed to live in the Highlands.

Would she ever make it to the Grants? She had discussed her situation many times with her mother. Her parents had been wonderful. They'd told her they would take her whenever she was ready to go, but not until the worst of the fighting was over.

Her mother wished to wait until Celestina's two brothers had made it home; this she understood. But Celestina's gut told her something bad had happened to someone special in her life, but whom? She changed her mind daily in trying to guess the identity of the injured party. On some days, she believed it to be Loki, on other days it was Brodie, but mayhap it was another of the Grant brothers?

The door flew open and she twirled toward the entryway. The guard who stood there said, "There's a wee lad asking for you at the gate, my lady. He is quite scruffy and we do no' wish to let him in without your approval."

She dashed toward the door. "Loki? Is it Loki?" Not waiting for an answer, she charged down the front steps and headed toward the gate, shouting Loki's name all the way. She must have appeared half-crazed, as everyone inside the inner bailey jumped out of her way.

She was hurrying through the gate when her father's bellow reached her ears. "Be careful, Celestina. Please wait for an escort."

But she could not. She hastened to the gate, toward the cluster of guards surrounding a small figure, tears running down her cheeks as she moved.

"Loki? Is it really you?" She pushed against a guard and fought her way to her dear little lad.

"Missy angel, missy angel!" Loki's wee arms flung wide as he threw himself at her.

"Here, now. No reason to make the lady as messy as you are, lad. Leave her be so you do no' cover her with your dirt and grime." One of the guards attempted to pull him away from her.

Celestina waved him off as she swung the wee lad into her embrace. "'Tis all right. I am not worried about a bit of dirt."

"Missy angel, listen to me. Stop hugging me and listen. Please!" Loki begged as he tugged on her sleeve.

Celestina's gut reeled as she set him down in front of her. "What is it?" she whispered, afraid to hear of what he had to say.

"Missy angel, 'tis Master Brodie."

Celestina's vision blurred and she thought she might faint. Nay, not her husband. She could not lose her husband. They were just getting to know each other. She fought to remain conscious so she could hear the rest of Loki's story.

"He is hurt, missy. Two Norsemen stabbed him in the leg and he bled and bled. Nicol is taking him home to the Highlands so his sister can fix him. The healer at the camp wanted to saw his leg off, but Laird Alex stopped him. He says Brenna will fix him and save his leg." Loki hesitated and took a deep breath.

The news made Celestina stumble, but she righted herself. He was alive. *Thank you, Lord, for saving my husband.* They could handle his injuries, whatever they were. He needed her. She should be by his side. Nay, she *had* to be by his side. She would leave immediately, she needed to make plans, but how would she get there?

"Come. I will take you there now."

Loki held his hand out and as soon as she placed her hand in his, he spun around, heading directly for the path. "Aye, Loki, take me to my husband. He needs me. I will be there for him." She searched the area for her parents so she could let them know of their plans.

A deep voice stopped both them in their tracks. "Whoa, lad. You have time to stay for something to eat and for us to help you prepare for your journey, aye?" Her father strode toward them, holding his hand out to Celestina.

She jerked in response to the large hand moving toward her, reflexively putting her hands in front of her face to defend herself.

Her father pulled his hand back, an alarmed expression on his face. "Och, lass. I will never raise a hand to you. 'Tis no' me. I love you and I am here to help you."

Celestina dropped her hands and nodded. This was her father, her true father, and she believed he would never hurt her deliberately.

He offered his hand again, this time keeping it a fair distance from her. She reached out and grabbed it, sighing in relief. He would be there for her.

Her father whispered. "Come, my dear, and we will find out all you need to know from the wee one, so we can help you find your husband. Remember, you are no longer alone; you have family to help you." Her father searched the area for strange horses but found none. He directed his next question to Loki. "Lad, how did you get here?"

Loki's panting slowed for a few seconds. "I ran."

Her father's shocked expression told her just how far they were from the battle. "You ran all the way alone?"

"Och, nay, I had some rides, but I ran from way back there!" His finger pointed toward the forest and the planting fields.

Ranald MacLaren strode over to Loki and patted him on the back. "Well done, lad. Now, come inside for something to eat, and we will make a plan. You can no' make it all the way into the Highlands without a horse and some provisions. See now, look at Celestina. Does she look ready to travel?"

Glancing from Celestina to The MacLaren, Loki finally answered, "Nay, Laird. I know how important it is for me to take care of Master Brodie's wife, so I will stay for a bit. And if you could spare me something to eat, I would be much obliged."

"Good decision. You must be a Grant warrior to think like that."

"Aye, Laird. I am, and I will be training with the warriors soon." Loki nodded his head in affirmation.

Celestina was so glad to see him. She smiled as they traipsed to the great hall, the boy's wee hand in hers, telling her again all he knew about Brodie's injury.

She had to get to the Grant clan to see her husband, but would her parents allow her to leave?

Chapter Twenty-Seven

Loki sees the Highlands and Grant land for the first time, something he'll never forget.

The wind blew colder and harsher the further they traveled. Celestina bundled the plaid around her as tight as it would go. She had given up the cart and now rode a horse alongside her father, her brother, Rory, and a few of the MacLaren guards. Her father had insisted her mother remain in the cart for protection against the bitterly cold Highland winds. Celestina had ridden with her for awhile to keep her company, but the trail was narrowing and her father had sent them on ahead while he stayed back with her mama. She had jumped at the chance to ride a horse and Inga had promised to keep her mother company.

Loki sat in front of her on her horse and offered guidance when it was needed. The lad had proven to be such a godsend, not least of all because he was adept at calming her worries. Her mind had thought of every possible situation they might find when they finally arrived at the Grant clan, but though everyone had chimed in to convince her Brodie was alive, it was Loki's quiet certainty that made her believe.

The beauty of the Highlands astounded her—the hills and waterfalls, the beautiful glens and valleys. As she shivered under her plaid, she swore that when she and her husband were reunited, she would force him to hold her in his warm embrace for hours until the chill moved out of her bones. No matter where they slept, be it under the stars or inside a cave, the nights were colder here than she'd ever imagined.

She lifted her face to the sun and breathed in the crisp autumn air, smiling because she could now understand why Brodie loved the Highlands so. This would be her home, and no matter how grievous his injury, they would work through it together. She would help him heal and be a good wife to him. She tried not to think sad thoughts because her tears tended to freeze on her face in the wind.

Instead, she turned her mind to her parents, who had supported her completely when she'd told them she could no longer wait to see her husband. She had offered to find someone to travel with in a cart, but her father had insisted on bringing her to the Grants himself, as had her mother.

The only one in their group more excited about their destination than Celestina was Loki. She pulled him in closer, hoping to keep him warm, though it seemed as though the wee sprite had more heat than she did.

The view became more breathtaking the further they traveled. Then, a few days after they had left, Loki grinned and tugged on her arm, his gloved finger pointing off into the distance. The largest castle she had ever seen graced a huge hill, surrounded by several rows of huts and thatched cottages and valleys with firths meandering through them. They could make out a loch to the left and fields to the side, though little grew at this time of year.

As they made their way, Celestina could make out the castle's parapets and the towers. Warriors were everywhere—walking the parapets, riding on horseback through the village, and practicing swordplay in the fields.

"Look, missy angel." Loki pointed to a field full of soldiers to the right of the castle. Swords reflected the sun as they swung in battle. "The lists! The famous Grant lists. Someday I will be able to practice there." His face lit up and he turned to her, grinning from ear to ear. She kissed his forehead and chuckled.

"Aye, I think you will, Loki."

The lad couldn't stop his chattering. "And look at that stone wall, 'tis the tallest ever. Naught will get past that! And see all the buildings inside the wall. I think I even see a chapel. The Grants have the biggest stable of all. Mayhap I can sleep there in the soft straw instead of on the ground."

His excitement was contagious. Her father's keep was large, but it was nothing like this.

Loki squeezed her hand. "'Twill no' be much longer, missy. We are almost there!" he shouted.

Epilogue

The end of Lucky Loki, and the beginning of a new life.

Brodie and Celestina made their way around the room, making sure everything was set for their surprise. The youngest members of the family, Bethia and Kyla, were upstairs with Jennie and Quade's younger sister, Avelina, who had promised to look after them. Loki had Alex and Maddie's twin lads under control near the back of the room with Torrian and his dog Growley and Lily.

After the toast to the bride and groom, hugs and

congratulations were exchanged across the room. Quiet finally descended as Laird Alexander Grant stepped to his dais and awaited everyone's attention.

"'Tis something else verra important that I must do today. I ask Lucky Loki to come forward, please."

Loki stared at the room full of people from the back of the great hall, clearly unsure of what to do.

"'Tis all right, lad," Alex said, beckoning him forward. "Torrian and Lily will watch the twins. You are needed up front."

As he crept forward, Loki's gaze searched for Celestina. Smiling at him, she nodded in encouragement.

Alex smirked when the lad stopped halfway across the room, staring at the Grant warriors in their plaids, unsure of where he was to go. "Closer, lad."

Once he had passed through the crowd, a group of Grant warriors gathered in a semi-circle behind him. Loki stood in front of Alex, his wee legs trembling.

Celestina's heart broke. Loki looked so lost standing in the middle of all those brawny warriors, especially since he was directly in front of the massive Laird Alex Grant. She worried the poor lad's neck would be sore from looking up at the tall Highlander. She had begged Brodie to allow her to stand next to him in support, but Brodie had refused.

Alex cleared his throat and began, his hands clasped behind his back. "Lucky Loki, do you understand the important code of the Grants, our values of both honor and truthfulness?"

A wee voice squeaked out just loud enough, "Aye, my laird."

"Lad, I have several questions to ask you and I only need you to answer 'aye' or 'nay.' Can you do that, son?"

Loki nodded.

"Is it true you snuck under a cart and rode in a hidden spot to follow Celestina?"

Loki, confused, glanced at Brodie before he answered. "Aye, my laird."

"Is it also true you caused pain to a servant of a nobleman by placing stones in his shoes without his knowledge?"

Loki's eyes widened. "Aye, my laird, but I was just trying…"

"Aye or nay, lad?" Alex barked.

He hung his head before answering, "Aye, my laird."

The laird continued. "Is it also true you ran from my brother's side and followed a cart out of town to find Celestina, without advising anyone of your destination?"

Loki's frantic gaze darted around the room, searching for support. "But, my laird, Celestina…"

"Aye or nay?" Alex's voice boomed through the hall.

"Aye, my laird," he said in a small voice.

Celestina couldn't take it any longer. She started toward the lad, just to let him know he was not alone, but her husband pulled her back and wrapped his arm around her waist.

"Trust our laird, *leannan*."

Celestina swiped at the tears in her eyes, leaning into her husband's embrace, but not before she noticed that Maddie, sitting by Alex's side in front of the dais, had a linen square at her face and was mopping up tears as well. She and Maddie were definitely kindred spirits.

Staring over Loki's wee head, Alex continued. "Is it true you went to the MacLaren keep by yourself, again without notifying anyone of your destination, just to let Celestina know her husband was injured?"

Loki's shoulders slumped, and he hung his head in shame. "Aye, my laird."

Alex's voice softened, "Is it no' also true, lad, that you stood proud and protected the Scots by using your slinger against the invaders?"

Lifting his gaze to meet Alex's, the boy said, "Aye, my laird."

"Is it true that after my wounded brother passed out from battle you managed to get him to the healer immediately?"

"Aye, my laird." His voice was now strong enough to be heard across the hall.

Alex smiled. "And did you no' use your sling to protect my sister-in-law, Celestina Grant, against a group of Norsemen in Lennox?"

The lad nodded his head, sniffling as he stared at Alex. "Aye, my laird."

Alex stepped down from the dais, grasped Loki's shoulders and said, "Well done, lad. You make me verra proud." Then he nodded to Brodie and Celestina, and they came to stand in front of Loki.

Loki's eyes grew big as saucers when Celestina pulled out the red and green Grant plaid made just for him and enfolded his wee body with it. Brodie approached his brother and handed Alex a small sword, then pinned a badge with the Grant crest on the wee lad's chest.

Their parts completed for now, Brodie and Celestina moved back to stand off to the side of Loki, and Alex moved closer to the lad. He positioned Loki where everyone could see him, then held his hand on the lad's shoulder. With his other hand, he touched the sword to Loki's head and began, "Lucky Loki, I christen thee a Grant. I am proud to say you acted as the fiercest Highlander in all the land, protecting the weak and innocent, acting with honor at all times, guarding a member of my family when necessary, and fighting bravely for our country."

When he finished, Alex handed the hilt of the sword to Loki, who took it into his trembling hands before Alex turned him to face the warriors behind him. Alex nodded his head, and the warriors who surrounded him unsheathed their swords at the same time, knelt in unison, each placing their weapon on the floor pointing toward Loki, individually pledging to protect him with their lives.

Celestina's tears flowed freely down her cheeks as she watched the expression of sheer wonder dance across Loki's face as the warriors knelt in front of him. Her husband wrapped his arms around her shoulders and tugged her in close for a quick kiss. After everything the lad had done for both of them, they were both so glad to see him receive this tribute.

When the warriors finished, Loki turned around, his face lit up with joy. He stared up at Alex and said, "I made it. Is that no' right, Laird Grant? Am I finally a Grant warrior and a member of your guard?"

Alex stood with his hands behind his back. "Nay, lad, that is no' correct."

Loki's face fell and his shoulders slumped. It was time. Brodie strode over to the lad's right side and Celestina to his left. Loki peered up at both of them, unsure of what was happening.

Alex cleared his throat. "Lad, I christened you a Grant, no' a Grant warrior. You will be asked to fight with the warriors, aye, but you are officially christened a Grant, with Celestina as your mama and Brodie Grant as your sire, if you will accept them as your parents in the eyes of Scottish law."

Loki looked first at Brodie, then at Celestina and said, "Truly, you want me?"

Brodie said, "Aye, lad, naught would make us happier than having you as our son. That is, if you want us."

Loki let out his best imitation of a Grant war whoop and jumped into Brodie's arms.

"Aye. I am no longer Lucky Loki."

Puzzled by his declaration, Celestina looked at him as he hopped down and ran to her side to hug her.

"I am Loki Grant," he said with a grin.

JOURNEY TO THE HIGHLANDS

BOOK 4

ROBBIE AND CARALYN

Loki became an important part of the clan, but most of all, he became the protector of the wee ones.

CHAPTER THIRTY-TWO

The man who controlled Caralyn was not about to let her go, so when Robbie took her away from him, he hired mercenaries to help him retrieve her. And the fools decided to abduct Caralyn's bairns. Big mistake with Loki and Growley around.

"CARALYN! GET TO the horses. Get the lasses on the horses!"

The sound of Quade's voice was enough to send a chill up her spine. She spun around and saw there were three horses headed straight for them. Malcolm. Malcolm with two others on horseback streaked across the meadow toward them.

Quade and Tomas jumped off the roof and mounted their own horses, readying themselves for a confrontation. Ashlyn screamed and started running toward the horses while Gracie was still headed toward Loki, oblivious to the approaching danger.

Caralyn dropped everything and raced for Gracie. *Oh Lord, help us.* She tore past Ashlyn, trying to reach Gracie. Only when it was too late did it occur to her that Ashlyn could not mount a horse on her own.

Tomas and Quade bellowed the Grant whoop as they galloped toward the intruders. Approaching the first horseman, Tomas swung his sword but missed. The second horsemen came behind him and swung a club and hit him in the back of his head, knocking him off his horse. Caralyn's gut clenched in panic when Tomas fell to the ground. Hard. *Get up, Tomas, get up*. He didn't move.

She picked up her skirts and raced as fast as she could, screaming at her girls to run. One man headed straight for Gracie, the other two headed toward her and Ashlyn.

Everything seemed to be moving in slow motion as her life fell apart in front of her. The smallest man leaned over and scooped Gracie up and the other grabbed Ashlyn by the arm and threw her across his horse. Caralyn changed direction and ran back toward the horses.

She glanced over her shoulder to see Loki come flying out of the bushes with Growley at his side. Both chased after the man with Gracie on his lap. Tears ran down her cheeks as she heard her daughters' screams rent the air. Quade went after Ashlyn, Loki after Gracie, and all Caralyn could do was try to get on her horse in an attempt to evade Malcolm.

As she mounted, Loki pulled his slinger out, loaded his stones into it, and pelted the man who held Gracie on his horse.

The lout yelled and slapped himself in the face. "My eye! The wee bastard hit me in my eye." He dropped Gracie and Loki ran over to pick her up, throwing her on the giant deerhound's back in one smooth movement, latching her arms around Growley's neck and her legs around his back. He then gave the dog a shove toward the trees and yelled, "Go, Growley!"

Growley hurtled down the path into the woods and Malcolm yelled at the brute. "Get her, you fool! Are you planning to let a wee lad beat you, Ray?"

Ray set off after Growley, but the dog ran in between bushes where the horse couldn't go. Gracie hung on for dear life, but she managed to stay on him, at least as far as Caralyn could see. *Go Growley, go!* Loki followed the attacker and continued to pepper him with his stones from behind. Ray finally cursed and turned his horse around, charging after Loki, who took off into the forest again, easily evading his pursuer.

Quade followed the brute who had Ashlyn flat across his horse in front of him, and managed to stab him through the back. The big man fell sideways, tumbling off the horse. The animal reared and Ashlyn grabbed its mane, screaming for help. Caralyn kneed her horse directing it toward Ashlyn.

Quade jumped off his horse and, after a quick battle, killed the one interloper who was still on the ground. When his horse returned, he mounted and took off after Ashlyn, finally grabbing the reins of the horse and scooping the girl onto his lap.

Caralyn gasped a sigh of relief. Both girls were safe for the moment. She surveyed the area and noticed Malcolm was now following her.

"Ray, go after the wean, you half-wit!" He pointed down the meadow where Growley had just emerged from the forest with Gracie still clutching his fur, her face buried in the hound's back.

Ray retreated and headed after Gracie again. She

watched in horror as Ray caught up with the dog and grabbed Gracie again just as Loki came tearing out of the woods.

Memories flooded Caralyn. In a matter of seconds, she saw the haunted look in Gracie's eyes change to joy at the Grant keep, Ashlyn's frown change to a smile as she played with Torrian, Jennie, and Avelina. She heard Robbie's chuckle as he stood at the hearth in the great hall with his brothers, Brodie and Alex.

And she made a decision. The choice had to be made quick, and she did not hesitate. She stopped her horse and held her arms out to Malcolm. "Leave my girls alone and I'll go with you willingly." She had no choice, her daughters were finally where they belonged. She wouldn't allow anything to take their happiness away. "Malcolm, leave Gracie behind and I'll go with you."

Malcolm smiled. "Let the wean go, Ray. I have what I want."

HIGHLAND SPARKS

BOOK 5

LOGAN AND GWYNETH

Logan and Gwyneth were a powerful couple, and everyone loved to watch their interplay.

CHAPTER EIGHT

Loki is chosen as a judge for a contest and meets Gwyneth.

IT WAS A glorious day, with a slight breeze that swirled the fallen leaves around her feet. She waited, pacing occasionally to help gather her strength, while the clan gathered off to the sides.

A voice broke into her thoughts and she looked up in time to see an exuberant Loki leaping and running across the field. "I'm one of the judges. My laird chose me."

She couldn't help but smile at the lad. "Does that surprise you, Loki?"

He came to a quick halt in front of her, gasping in excitement. "Aye. I just became a Grant."

Gwyneth's brow furrowed as she stared at the lad. She had heard part of his story, but not everything.

"You see, I used to live in a crate behind the tavern in Ayr, and Brodie Grant found me, and I helped him find missy angel, Celestina, and then we saved missy angel from the surly pig-nut—" his eyes grew wide as he swung his fist in the air, "—and we fought the mean Norse together, but I had to get my sire to the healer 'cause he was wounded." He paused to take a breath. "Then I went to tell my mama Brodie was wounded, but she wasn't my mama yet." He stopped to point at Celestina and gave her a huge grin. Tipping his head to the side, his hand came up to his mouth in thought. "I… helped her come here and…." He stopped, a scowl across his face as if he had missed something in his tale. His face lit up. "Then my laird had a 'ficial cereminny and made me a Grant. So now I have a sire, Brodie Grant, and a mama, and I am Loki Grant." He pounded his chest with a smile.

"After this contest, I'd like to hear more about that. Tell me, you don't have a problem with a lass beating a lad, do you, Loki Grant?" She smirked as he stared at her, his eyes wide.

"Nay, my lady. I will vote for whoever is best. I promise to be honest. 'Tis part of being in the Grant clan. I must always tell the truth."

Gwyneth ruffled his hair. "I trust you will, lad. Why don't you check the targets to make sure everything is set up properly?"

"I will, my lady." Loki yelled back over his shoulder as he took off down the field.

THE BRIGHTEST STAR IN THE HIGHLANDS

BOOK 7

JENNIE AND AEDAN

Loki always had a wee crush on Jennie, and Alex Grant was glad of it.

CHAPTER TEN

Loki takes care of his wee brother but also protects Jennie, claiming his role as protector.

DONNAL INTERRUPTED. "IF it pleases you, Laird Grant, I would like to insist on a wedding before the next moon, as we are in need of some organization at our castle. Seems our staff have become quite slovenly and lazy. We need someone who can crack the whip, shall I say?" His smug expression did not speak well for him.

A small commotion took place over in the bairn's area, so Maddie promptly got up to tend to them.

"Truly, Laird," Donnal said, glancing over his shoulder at the unruly group. "Is there a reason you have the weans nearby? Are they not too young to act appropriately around guests?"

"Aye, there is a reason," Alex said gruffly. "They're my weans and I want them here. They'll learn to act appropriately in time."

Jennie stifled a giggle, wishing she could hug her brother over his declaration. He was a good sire and a good leader.

"Mama!" Braden screamed. Maddie whispered something soft in his ear, then sent Loki away with him.

"You see. They are too young." He nodded his head, apparently in affirmation of his previous statement, but no one volunteered to agree with him.

"That wean is my brother's first born lad, and I prefer to have him here. Please do not concern yourself, Boyd."

Donnal let out a loud belch and excused himself. "Must find the garderobe."

Coll reached for her hand under the table. "My apologies for his rudeness. 'Tis unforgiveable. I love weans and hope to have many."

Jennie turned to look into his kind eyes—he was such a better lad than the other suitor—but she still pulled her hand back. She noticed Donnal was headed in the same direction as Loki. Her intuition told her to follow them so she excused herself and did just that, trailing him toward the passageway that led to the tower rooms where Brodie and Celestina lived.

Once she left the great hall, she caught sight of Donnal a few steps behind Loki, who was desperately trying to manage an unruly Braden.

"Here, lad. I'll handle the wee twit." Donnal reached for Braden, but his wee protector was faster.

Loki pulled his small sword from his sheath. The weapon connected with the skin of the suitor's hand and drew a drop of blood, causing him to yank it back. "You will remove your hand from my brother, my lord. No one touches him without my permission."

"Why, you ungrateful cur."

Jennie rushed up to them just as Donnal was about

to wrest away Loki's sword. "Leave him be, my lord. They are not bothering anyone."

He spun around to glare at her. "They're bothering me. Weans should not be heard from. They should know their place."

Jennie nodded to Loki. "Why do you not continue and take Braden to his mama."

"Nay, I will not leave you unprotected with this brute, Lady Jennie." His chin came up and he squared his shoulders, just like his sire did so many times, his sword still drawn at his side. Braden had stopped crying and was staring at the stranger with wide eyes.

Jennie smiled. "My thanks, Loki, but I can handle myself."

Loki nodded and continued on his way, tugging a whining Braden behind him, but he watched Jennie over his shoulder. Loki had grown quite a bit over the last couple of years, and he was mighty protective of his adopted family.

Chapter Fourteen

You just never know where you'll find Loki next.

Jennie strolled along with Ennis, taking the turn toward Brenna's garden, away from the crowd in the bailey. She trusted Ennis more than her first two suitors combined, and she had to agree with Brodie. Perhaps it was good for her to compare men. Ennis MacKenzie happened to be the only other man who'd captured her interest to any degree, so why not see how it felt to be in his arms?

"May I call you Jennie? And please call me Ennis."

"Of course."

"Jennie, I would love to bring you to my home to meet my mother. She would enjoy talking about healing with you."

Jennie rubbed the back of her neck. Hellfire, but the dancing had heated her up. Sweat dripped underneath her hair. She knew it was not quite ladylike to be dripping with sweat, so she tried to wipe it away.

"Would you be agreeable to discussing such an arrangement with your brother?"

Jennie glanced into his kind eyes. "I only just arrived home, so I am not quite ready to travel yet. Mayhap in a sennight or so."

She wasn't ready to leave while Aedan was here. That was the truth of the matter. Ennis was nice, but there was something different between her and Aedan, something special. She needed to discover if Aedan had any interest in her at all, and if she left for MacKenzie land now, there was a possibility that she would never see him again.

Nay, she had to stay here for a while. Somehow, Jennie was just now noticing that they had wandered quite a ways from the main path. The sky around them was dark, and Ennis had managed to maneuver her under a big tree. Before she knew it, her back was pressed against the trunk of the tree, and one of his hands had settled on her shoulder.

His lips descended on hers, and she allowed it. He tried to angle his mouth against hers to force her lips apart, but she denied him because it just wasn't the same. It wasn't bad, but it wasn't enticing either.

He was a fine lad. The problem was that he wasn't Aedan.

Suddenly, a loud growl met her ears. She jumped back just in time to see Aedan grab Ennis by the back of the neck and hurl him across the stone path, where he landed in a stunned heap on the ground.

"What the hell, Cameron!" he bellowed. "Tend to your own affairs."

But Aedan threw himself on top of Ennis, his fist flying and connecting with the other man's face. "Jennie's mine. Do not *ever* touch her again."

Another loud whoop rent the air, and something dropped out of the tree next to the two of them.

Loki. He came to a stop next to the two men. In moments, his sword was out and aimed at MacKenzie.

"You can both stay away from my aunt," Loki growled.

"Loki, stop! Aedan, cease!" Jennie shouted just as Brodie came down the pathway.

"Hellfire. Jennie? Loki? What goes on here? I heard Loki's whoop just as I walked outside." Brodie stood with his arms crossed and his legs planted.

All other movement had come to a halt since Loki still brandished his sword at the grappling men, forcing them to put a stop to their fighting. "Get up," Brodie said to the two men on the ground.

Aedan stood and moved to Jennie's side. "Are you all right?"

"Aye." She stared at him. "I'm fine. What is the meaning of this?"

"Defending your honor. He had his hands where they didn't belong."

Ennis jumped to his feet and brushed off his clothing, a sheepish expression on his face. "My apologies. I did not do anything against the lady's will."

Brodie quirked his brow at Jennie. "Jennie? Would you care to explain yourself?"

Jennie sputtered, realizing she had put herself in a very uncomfortable position. "Please. 'Tis over. Can we let everything go?"

Loki shouted, "Hellfire! He had his hands all over her. He needs to pay." He moved his sword so the point was close to MacKenzie's throat.

Ennis rolled his eyes. "Truly, Grant? This is ridiculous."

Brodie glowered at him. "Is it?"

Loki's face glowed red with anger, his eyes lit with a fury Jennie had never seen. "You do not come to your friends' land and assault their sister…or their aunt. We shall see what my laird has to say about this."

"Loki, lower your sword." Brodie's hand settled on his hips.

"Must I? They deserve something." Loki gripped his sword until his knuckles were white.

"Loki!" Brodie said through clenched teeth. "I know you are the great protector of all our lasses and bairns, but I think Jennie can handle herself."

Loki's head dropped and he did as he was instructed. "Someday, you'll appreciate my protecting."

"I already have, lad, as you are aware. Go back inside."

Loki shuffled off toward the keep, his shoulders

slumped. He peered over his shoulder once to give Jennie a forlorn look, but then continued onward.

Chapter Fifteen

Jennie lets Loki down as nicely as she can…

When Jennie stepped inside the keep, she searched for Loki. She finally found him over in a secluded corner, his shoulders slumped as he stared at the crowd of people chatting inside.

"Loki?"

His face lit up when he saw her. "Jennie. My apologies for interfering, but I do not like those men."

Jennie sat on a nearby bench and patted the seat next to her. Loki sat down, hanging his head.

"I cannot believe you are almost as tall as I am. When did that happen?"

His eyes danced and he grinned as he peered up at her, clearly pleased she had noticed he was getting older.

"My thanks for being my protector," she added. "I am new at being around lads, since Alex has protected me for so long."

"Aye, well, you still need to be protected. He was doing things he should not have been doing." Loki frowned and stared at his feet.

"'Tis true he kissed me, but I allowed it."

"Why? Can you not see he is wrong for you?" he said, his brow furrowed.

"Aye, now I do. But I needed to find out for myself. You are growing up too fast for me, Loki.

Not long ago, you would have called him a surly pig-nut."

Loki laughed. "I did like that name. Ennis isn't surly." He gazed into her eyes. "Must you choose someone?"

Ah, Brodie had been correct in his assessment of Loki's affections. She thought for a moment before she spoke again. "Alex is not forcing me to choose, but I do wish to marry. There was a time when I loved my brothers more than I could love any other man. Do you know, I always thought of you as my brother instead of my nephew? You are much older and more mature than the lads that are about. I feel as if I have four brothers, all looking out for me."

"Aye, 'tis true." He nodded and waited for her to continue.

"Do you know that I once wished on a star that you would grow up fast enough to be my age so we could marry?" Mayhap he would feel better about their parting with this explanation. She remembered having numerous crushes when she was young. No matter how old, rejection always hurt.

"You did?" His eyes widened.

"Aye, I did." She paused, giving Loki time to grasp her meaning. "I knew you would be a perfect husband."

"But I did not grow any faster, did I?" His face dropped, and he stared at the floor.

"'Tis good we are not able to marry."

He gave her a puzzled look. "But why?"

"Because we are family, and family stays close forever. Besides, if I chose you, too many lassies would have their hearts broken."

Loki snickered. "Truly? You made that up."

"Did I? Now that Alex has invited the rest of the clan inside to enjoy the dancing, have you taken the time to look about you? If you had, you would have noticed all the lassies who cannot take their eyes from you. They would be quite upset if you married me."

Loki yanked his gaze from hers and searched the hall for the truth of her words. "But they look at you, Jennie."

"Nay, lad. Do you see the one with the freckles and the golden hair? And the one with the dark plait in the dark red gown? And the one in dark blue near your sire? Allow me to turn my head. Trust me, if you smile at them, they will return your smile."

She turned her head away to give Loki the chance to look at the lasses she had pointed out to him. He beamed when he turned back to face her. "'Tis true. Each one smiled at me."

"Loki, you have grown up to be a handsome lad, and what's more important, you are honorable and hard-working. The lasses will soon be chasing you wherever you go."

"I like the lass with the yellow hair."

"Why don't you talk to her? Never mind, here comes your mama with a wailing Braden. He wants his favorite brother. Do you know he prefers you over everyone?"

"Aye." He grinned. "I am pleased to have a brother."

"And a big sister."

He stared at her, confused.

"Me. My thanks for protecting me like a brother.

I'll be safe for the rest of the night. I will always trust Aedan Cameron, but I am glad you followed me with Ennis. I really do not know him well."

He thought for a moment before he nodded and ran off to join his mother and Braden.

Chapter Eighteen

Loki the savior…

Way off in the distance came a lone rider. He had stayed to the rear, close enough to make sure he was aware of everything that transpired, but not close enough to be seen and suspected of wrongdoing. He would not be successful in his mission if he did not know the others' plan.

And he had to be successful. He was the savior. Someday they would understand his purpose, but not yet. The Grant lass was the true treasure.

Thus far, everything had worked perfectly. He would be successful, without a doubt.

He grinned in triumph and returned to his hiding place.

Chapter Twenty-One

Someone has to save Jennie!

The Savior's patience paid off. He waited until Dermid left for the Cameron keep. Then he needed to wait just a few more moments until the fool guarding Jennie Grant fell asleep. He was quite certain it would take less than an hour for that to happen.

He kept an eye on Cameron's wife, making sure

she was not hurt or ill. It was obvious she was uncomfortable, and he could almost smell the stench of the cloth they'd used to gag her from his spot, but no matter. She would have to tolerate it a bit longer. He had no intention of taking the gag from her mouth after he captured her. She would be spewing curses at him, endangering both of their lives, so it would stay until he played his part and finished this whole escapade.

He searched the surrounding area through the tree branches, but did not see Dermid anywhere. They were quite alone in this hidden area, though it was clearly not as well hidden as the kidnappers believed it to be since he had found his way here.

Once he had checked in all four directions, he took a deep breath and aimed.

He jumped from the treetop directly onto Dermid's accomplice, taking the lout by surprise. The savior beat the man's face, pummeling him with his fists, then pulled his sword from its sheath and held it at his throat.

The daft fool reached for him anyway, forcing him to cut his throat and end his life.

Then the savior turned to the victim, smiled, and reached for her.

Jennie hollered but the gag muffled her shouts. No matter. He had a mission to complete, so he lifted her and tossed her over his shoulder, though it took a wee bit for him to steady himself. Once he reached the fool's horse, he placed her over the horse and mounted behind her.

Jennie struggled and fought to loosen her ties, but the savior shouted, "Cease!"

His mission was almost done.

The savior traveled through the early night, certain of his destination. He hated to keep his captive tied and gagged across his horse, but it was paramount that they travel without making much noise. He had no idea where Dermid MacLean had gone, and didn't wish to attract attention.

When he was certain they were out of danger, he stopped his horse and pulled the gag out of Jennie's mouth.

Jennie shouted, "Loki Grant, what the hell were you doing leaving me tied up?"

Loki's shoulders straightened and his chin jutted out. "I did what my training as a Grant warrior taught me to do. I got you out of danger before freeing you. Here, give me your hands and I'll undo your bindings."

"You did not need to keep me tied up, I could have helped you. I know the area better than you. I could have kept an eye out for Dermid. I could have helped…"

"Shush! This is why I left you tied. Could you cease for a moment so we can make a plan? If you keep your barking, Dermid will hear you from the other side of Cameron land. I am only doing what my sire taught me. You must stay observant and not make your move until you are certain of success. You are safe, are you not?"

Jennie looked at Loki and started giggling. Once unbound, she sat up on the horse and turned to face him. "My thanks for saving me, Loki." She threw her arms around him. "You scared me half to death when you jumped out of the tree, but I was verra glad to see you."

He hugged her back, but then held his finger to his lips. "Hush. Listen!"

A bellowing yell echoed across the small glen they were in. Jennie turned to Loki and said, "Alex. I would know his shout anywhere." She shifted in the saddle and said, "That way. We will be sure to catch him."

Epilogue

And his special talents are recognized again, this time by a lass named Arabella.

This was to be their last night on Grant land before they headed home on the morrow. Jennie had told Aedan more about Loki's background and how he had ended up joining the family. With Alex and Maddie's approval, they had requested this special night to include all the guards and their families.

After a filling meal and before the revelry was to start, Alex kissed Maddie's cheek and then moved to the front of the dais and waited for the crowd to settle. Robbie and Brodie ushered everyone to the side and to the back while Aedan got up and stood beside Alex.

The Grant cleared his throat. Once the crowd's whispers about the event settled, Alex placed his hands behind his back. "I call Loki Grant forward."

Loki made his way to the front and stood in front of Alex, just as he had done a long time ago, still looking quite small next to the huge Alexander Grant. While he had grown, his surprise still made him look young and innocent.

"Loki Grant, 'tis with great pride that I celebrate your efforts in saving my sister, Mistress of the Cameron Clan, from the hands of a mad man. You are a braw warrior and I am proud to have you as a nephew and a valued member of our clan. The Chieftain of the Camerons has something he wishes to say."

Aedan nodded to his guards, who formed a line behind Loki Grant, then did a short drill with their swords before lining up behind Loki once more.

He removed something from his pocket and held it up for all to see. "I bestow this jeweled brooch as a gift from my clan, the Camerons, unto Loki Grant. It carries our crest, and while we recognize that Loki is part of the Grant clan, he is also an honorary member of the Cameron clan. For those of you who do not know of his heroism, he chose to make himself my wife's guardian, and in so doing, saved her life."

He turned to Jennie and handed her the brooch. She walked toward Loki, who was now the same height as she was, though still growing, and pinned it next to his Grant brooch. She hugged him and then stood back, holding her hand up to make an announcement of her own.

"You may have heard the story, but not my version. I was hit over the head, and while I was unconscious, I was bound and gagged and stuffed into a burlap sack. When I awoke, I was in an area I had never seen before, and I listened to two men discuss my fate. They planned to use me as bait for my husband, then leave me to die, bound and gagged, where I would have definitely succumbed to the elements.

"Once the sack was removed, I could see my captors, but I could see no way out. Fortunately for me, Loki had followed my captors and hid in a tree without making a sound. He fell on a man twice his size, killing him in order to save me."

The group gasped in unison, some nodding at the story they had already heard.

Loki, embarrassed at being the center of attention, fiddled with his fingernails.

"My thanks to you, Loki, for being my guardian. You are a verra special member of my family, and I will treasure you always." She hugged him before stepping back.

Alex and Cameron stepped down from the dais while the crowd continued to applaud Loki. The minstrels and musicians came in, and all made ready for dancing.

Some time later, when she was alone, Loki found his way over to her.

"Aye, Loki?"

He struggled for words, but finally said, "I want you to know…I want to say…You were correct before. I did have feelings for you, but not anymore. Well, now I have different feelings. I realize our ties as family are much more important, and I also want you to know that I followed you because you are like my sister, not for any other reason."

Jennie smiled. "I know. We are family, Loki."

"I like the Cameron. I will miss you, but I think you chose well, and I wish you much happiness."

She hugged him and said, "My thanks."

Directly behind him, three young lassies about his age stood gazing at him in awe. Jennie took a step back, trying not to laugh. Loki turned around to face them, a puzzled expression on his face.

The first lass said, "Loki, you are such a strong guard."

The second lass said, "Loki, you are so handsome."

The first two lasses ran away, giggling.

The third lass, a girl with reddish-gold curls and a spattering of freckles across her nose, stepped up to him, took a deep breath, and declared, "Loki Grant, you are the handsomest, most braw warrior I have ever seen. Someday, I'm going to marry you." She leaned toward him, closed her eyes, and pressed her lips against his.

Jennie did not move, not wanting to ruin Loki's moment.

When the lass ended the kiss, she whispered, "My name is Arabella, and I promise to love you forever." She twirled around and ran away.

Loki turned to Jennie, blushing a deep red.

"Verra nice, Loki." Jennie said, her eyebrows raised. "I think she's quite bonny."

Loki broke out into the biggest grin she had ever seen.

"I like her. Someday, I'll make her my wife."

YULETIDE ANGELS

BOOK 9

CHAPTER SEVEN

Maddie makes poor decisions, but Loki saves the day again.

"GOD'S BONES, IT'S not like she has many choices, Grant. She would take the ravine because 'tis faster," Logan shouted.

Alex had been arguing with him over which way Mac would have taken Maddie.

"It's faster, aye, but not nearly as safe. Would Mac have risked it?"

"With Maddie hastening him, I'd say he would have. They would have been here earlier, before this heavy snowfall."

"The wind is strengthening, and we'll be in a full storm before long," Alex said.

Brodie nodded. "We need to cross the ravine before that. We'll not be able to see where we're going soon, and it's a long fall down if we attempt it then."

Alex nodded, silently cursing his wife's stubborn nature. Or was it his own stubborn nature that was at fault this time? He'd not explained his reasoning well, instead expecting Maddie to do whatever he said without question. Brenna had warned him once that his ideas were outmoded and daft at times.

His thoughts were interrupted when he noticed a horse coming toward them.

He knew Logan saw the same, because he pointed toward it in the distance and said, "Here comes the missing lad. Mayhap he has news for us."

Loki's horse galloped straight toward them, the lad's excitement visible even from a distance.

Brodie yelled out to him, "I'll chastise you later for going off on your own, but what have you for us? You've discovered something, have you not?"

"Aye," he said, pausing to catch his breath. "They went through the ravine. I checked which way they were going, then came back to tell you. I'll bet they're in the cave by now."

"Aye, if Mac is wise enough not to listen to my stubborn wife, who I'm sure wanted to press on." Alex cursed under his breath again, then remembered to thank Loki. "I'm pleased you were so resourceful, lad."

Logan said, "She'll stop in the cave, Grant. Her goal was to get far enough that you'd have to take her to Ramsay land. And as you said before, she's not used to traveling for that long. She'll be freezing."

"I'm not sure that cave would be considered halfway," Alex said, his lips pursed tight to keep himself from launching into another tirade. How the hell could Maddie have done something so foolish? No matter how he tried, he couldn't come up with any sound reason for her to act so rashly with their bairns and Alice and Mac. Being foolish over her own comforts was one thing, but to risk the young and the elderly was beyond something he thought her capable of doing. Even if he had ordered her around, she knew better.

Logan snorted. "After several hours in this weather with three bairns, she'll be wishing it's more than halfway."

Alex cast a sideways glance at Logan, knowing he was right.

Still, his concern over how they were faring in this storm only grew. He worried especially for Kyla and Alice.

"Let's move on. Loki, lead the way."

The Highland Clan 1280

LOKI

BOOK 1

Loki's story grabbed everyone's heartstrings, but as he grew up on Grant land, he learned that not everyone there thought he had the right to be treated as a member of Clan Grant. Discrimination for those who were different, medieval style.

CHAPTER ONE

Loki wants to marry his beloved Arabella, but her father disapproves, so he sets out to prove his worth with the help of Logan and Gwyneth.

LOKI GRANT OPENED one eye and the first thought that passed through his mind was: *Who am I*? The strangest thing about that was it was the one question he could not answer. He knew his name, but what else did he know?

He closed his eyes again as pain from his head rippled through him. He reached up with one hand to feel the swelling by his eye and the giant egg on his head. Rolling onto his side, he placed his hands on the cold, hard ground beneath him and pushed up with a roar loud enough to send the few birds left in the Highlands squawking off to another tree.

A voice came from off to his side, a voice he knew and trusted but couldn't quite place yet.

"How's the head feel? Like you are daft and have no sense? If so, then you have the right of it. You have no sense at all. How many, or do you not remember?" Logan Ramsay, his uncle, chuckled at him. Actually, Logan wasn't truly his uncle, but his Aunt Brenna had married into the Ramsay family, and the bonds between the two families were so strong that he considered the man an uncle. Loki managed to turn his head to stare at Logan, who was seated on the log next to him.

Logan held his hand out, offering him a bit of ale from a skin.

Loki took it, groaning again. "Arseholes. Every one of them."

"How many?"

"Five."

"When the hell are you going to stop trying to get yourself killed, fool? I've taught you better than that. You're interested in working for the Scottish crown like I do, and I'm happy to teach you. I'd like you to take over some of my jobs so I can spend more time at home with my Gwynie before I die. I'm not getting any younger, but you are not getting any smarter, are you?"

Loki took another slug of the ale before handing it back to his uncle. "How did you know where to find me?"

"People talk. Even reivers. They all talked about the tall fool who thought he could take on five men. When will you learn?"

"The news we heard about my sire was wrong. There was no information to be found about him anywhere near Ayr. The lad who gave us that information must have been daft. I was about to return to the Highlands when the reivers set upon me. I'm practicing everything you've taught me, Uncle."

"Apparently not. I've taught you that the most valuable weapon you have is your head, yet you keep getting it beaten. You'll have no brains left if you keep going on in this manner."

When a rustling from the forest reached his ears, he jumped up and grabbed for his dagger, though he came up with naught. Logan's wife, Gwyneth, emerged from the trees a moment later, her boots crunching on the thin layer of snow on the ground. "Leave off, Logan. He'll have enough pain without you making it worse. Loki, where are you hurt besides your head?"

Loki paced in a circle, moving about awkwardly at first, but then settling into a limp.

"How old are you, lad?" Logan asked, his green eyes narrowing.

"How in hell would I know the answer to that?"

"Dinna rail at me. How old did your mother and father decide you were when they found you and took you in?"

"Seven or eight summers. Would make me twenty and four or five."

"Well, you look and act like you're an auld man. You better start using that quick mind of yours or you'll soon be in trouble. There is no call to lose your head because you could not find your sire. You knew 'twould not be easy."

"Enough, Logan. Let him get his bearings before you chew his arse out." Gwynie made her way over to Loki, carrying a wet linen she'd presumably brought from the creek.

"I do not need it. My thanks." Loki Grant had two goals in life—to find his true parents and to marry Arabella Lewis. At this point, he faced failure on both fronts. Despite his best efforts, he could not find his sire. Thus he could not prove his worth to Bella's father, who would not allow his daughter to marry a man of uncertain blood. This trip had been intended for a dual purpose—to begin training to work for the Scottish crown and to search for his sire. This most recent experience had forced him to concede to the impossible. Since he could not measure up to Bella's father's standards, he might as well leave the clan and work for the Scottish crown as his aunt and uncle had done for years. But he knew Bella, the love of his life, would not be happy about his decision even though he'd attempted to get her ready for the possibility by telling her this trip was to train for work with the crown.

The truth was he didn't wish to tell her he'd failed again on obtaining the information necessary to make their marriage possible.

Gwyneth held out the cloth and charged toward him. "I'm cleaning it, whether or not you wish it. You're not thinking clearly yet. Now hold still." Gwyneth set to work on him, not speaking during her ministrations. His aunt had the magic intuition of knowing when to speak and when to keep quiet. Her dark leggings and forest green tunic, her favorite colors, almost made her melt into their surroundings. Still as thin as a young lass, she was agile and tough. Whereas most lasses he knew were proficient at needlework, his aunt was a renowned archer and hunter.

Loki did as he was told. He loved his aunt and uncle as much as he loved the rest of his adopted family. His real mother or father had left his life, for whatever reason, too early for him to recollect either one of them. Brodie Grant, his adopted sire, had found him living in a crate behind a tavern, and the two had worked together to save Brodie's new wife, Celestina. Afterwards, the young couple had brought him back to the Highlands and accepted him as their son. Loki adored them both for all they had done for him, and someday, he hoped to be able to tell them how much, especially his mama, but not yet. He didn't know why, but whenever he tried to express his love and gratitude, it was as if he turned mute.

But while his adopted family never made him feel less than accepted, other members of the clan liked to remind him that he was not truly of Grant blood. Now it was his job to prove himself to everyone, but he was still making a fool of himself. When Gwyneth finished cleaning the dried blood off his face and placed some salve on him, she said, "You know, you do not have to do this. You'd be happier if you stayed at the Grant castle in the Highlands. 'Tis where you belong. We all know it but you."

Loki nodded his thanks for her ministrations, then stalked off into the woods to relieve himself. Once finished, he found a nearby creek and knelt down to throw some ice cold water on his face, pausing to wash his hands and neck as well. He had few memories of the battle, only that five men on horseback had stolen all his weapons and his horse and knocked him out.

He'd failed again. Mayhap his aunt was right, and it was finally time to head back home to the Highlands—only to leave forever. He returned to the clearing and shrugged his shoulders at Logan.

"My decision is made. I'll return to inform my parents that I'll be working for the crown from here on out. Then I'll meet you wherever you would like to complete my training. I'll not go searching for my sire again."

"Loki," Gwyneth said, "I think you're making the right choice about your sire. You have two adoptive parents who love you. Give up on your true parents. You may never know, and there's no point in allowing it to ruin your life. But are you sure you do not wish to reconsider and marry Bella?"

"I cannot, Gwyneth. Her father will not allow it. So I'd rather leave and work for the crown than see her marry another. Will you train me?" He glanced from Gwyneth to Logan, feeling the defeat weigh down his entire body. All his sword work, all the careful training and eating he'd done to increase his size and his muscles, suddenly taunted him. As a young lad, all he'd desired had been to train as a Grant warrior, to live in the Highlands and fight like the renowned Alexander Grant, his uncle, and now that he was close to accomplishing that goal, it had lost all its power over him. Perhaps he should have done something entirely different with his time.

Logan nodded his head. "Aye, we'll train you. Gwynie can ride with me. We'll go with you to your keep."

"Mayhap we can stop at Drummond or Cameron land and get a horse. That way you can have a shorter journey home."

"Nay," Logan snorted. "We'll travel with you all the way home. Your father would have my arse if I let you ride alone, looking like a lad with no brain to use his brawn. Then, when you're ready, we'll leave together. You'll just have to stop at Clan Ramsay for a bit afterwards."

Rather than argue, Loki climbed onto one of the horses and flicked the reins.

Logan helped Gwynie mount and climbed up behind her, wrapping his plaid around the both of them. Silently, Loki cursed himself for having made them come out in such cold weather. It was not quite winter yet, so they could still navigate, but it would not be the best of treks through the Highlands at this time of year. He'd try to talk them out of following him the entire way later. He didn't have the energy right now.

"Did you find out anything at all about your true sire?" Gwyneth asked.

"Nay." Loki frowned. "I really do not care any longer. I've ended my search."

"Whenever you change your mind," Gwyneth said, giving him a knowing look, "we'll be glad to help again."

"My thanks," Loki muttered. It was hopeless. He'd never find out who he truly was and why he'd been living in a crate at seven summers in the royal burgh of Ayr.

His interest in his past had finally been beaten out of him.

Chapter Two

How he dreaded telling his adoptive mother, the pain in her eyes too much for him.

He stepped inside the door to a large chorus of greetings. He waved to all the friends and family gathered in the great hall, then turned to the right to head toward the corner passageway that led to the tower rooms, the place where his parents lived. His uncle had continued to expand the keep, eventually adding another building of chambers due to the swelling size of their immediate clan, but his parents had remained in the towers—the most comforting place in the world as far as Loki was concerned, mostly because of his mother. He continued down the passageway, wondering how his parents had been. He grimaced and reminded himself that he was thinking of his *adopted* parents.

He'd been so fortunate to be adopted by Brodie and Celestina Grant, no one knew it better than he did. So why had he risked hurting them by seeking out his true parents? Even though they had never said so, he could tell how much it wounded his mother by the look that came into her eyes every time he mentioned searching for his real parents. He could not tolerate that look. In fact, every time he saw it, he turned away, feeling so guilty he wanted to run in the opposite direction. If not for Arabella's foolish sire, he would never have tried to seek out his true sire. He believed he was a lad of value, but there was no way of proving his lineage.

Celestina's English father had kept her locked up in their house as a young lass. Loki had first set eyes on her as she sobbed from the balcony of her home, basically her prison. Being wee at the time, he could sneak anywhere without being seen. So he had followed Celestina, his 'missy angel,' as he had referred to her, wherever life took her. It was this sneakiness that had earned him the admiration of Brodie Grant, the youngest brother to Laird Alexander Grant, for it had helped Brodie to find her after she was kidnapped, right before the Battle of Largs.

After the conflict ended, Brodie and Celestina were reunited in the Highlands, and it was then they had adopted Loki and brought him into their home. He still counted the day he became Loki Grant as the happiest—and luckiest—day in his life.

He opened the doorway to the tower chambers and stepped inside.

A chorus of "Loki!" greeted him. His mother sat with her needlework in her lap, but she stood as soon as she laid eyes on him, dropping her sewing onto a nearby stool. Her expression had gone from sadness to excitement in an instant. His two sisters, Catriona and Alison, twelve and five summers, ran up and hugged him. His brother, Braden, would be in the lists with his father.

His mother waited for him to come to her, as she always did—a relic of her proper English manners. With a still trim figure and long yellow hair threaded with only a few strands of silver, Celestina Grant was still a beauty. Some of his aunts had widened at the hips after carrying bairns, but not his mother. She was still the most beautiful woman in the Highlands.

But that wasn't really what he saw. To him, she was

simply the woman with the biggest heart he had ever known. She held her arms wide and he stepped into her embrace, towering over the wee woman.

"Loki, how I have missed you." She patted his shoulders. "I am so glad to see you." She stepped back and cupped his cheek. "How do you fare? Did you find your true parents?"

And that look of excitement in her gaze changed to one of worry as fast as could be. Just the mention of the identity of his true parents was enough to send heartache through his adopted mother. Loki chastised himself, as he'd already done countless times already. He could never love his birth mother as he loved Celestina. Someday, he promised himself, he would tell this woman how much her love had meant to him.

It had all been for Bella—to prove to her father that he was not some worthless orphan. True, his uncle could force the marriage, but it would feel wrong to allow his powerful adoptive relatives to fight his battles for him. Since he'd been so long without parents, he wanted Bella's relationship with her sire to be strong. He had no desire to cause any discord between the two. Someday, he hoped he and Bella would have their own bairns, and bairns needed their grandparents, just as he had needed parents of his own.

But he had searched and searched, turning up naught. Now it was time to give up.

Chapter Five

Loki meets Kenzie behind a familiar inn…

Logan, Loki, and Torrian set out the next day with several guards. Gwyneth had chosen to stay home with the bairns since she had been journeying across the Highlands for a time. They arrived at the outskirts of the village toward the end of the day. As they paid the toll to enter into the royal burgh of Ayr, chills ran down Loki's spine. This was where his sire had found him. He had not been in Ayr proper since the Battle of Largs in the 1260s, when the Scots had gained the Western Isles back from Norway. Exhausted, he glanced at Torrian, who seemed awed by the place. He was surprised his Uncle Quade had allowed Torrian on this excursion, but Logan had pressured his brother into agreeing, arguing that it would not only be an opportunity for Torrian to meet King Alexander, but for him to learn some basic survival skills.

Loki was so exhausted that he was starting to have strange flashes in his brain. Visions of past experiences that he could not quite identify popped into his mind. People without faces in unfamiliar settings called to him, but naught and no one was recognizable. As soon as they rode past a certain spot at the edge of the burgh, he stopped his horse and called out to his uncle and cousin, asking them to give him a minute.

He dismounted in front of a dingy inn, one for the travelers with few coins. He stood in front of it and stared. The inn his father had found him behind was a place much like this one. Bits and pieces came back to him, memories he had chosen to forget. Logan asked him a question, but he ignored it. Driven by an unknown force, he stepped to the back of the building and found what he'd been seeking.

A crate.

He nudged the crate with his foot, and it moved just a touch, enough for him to see there were items inside the crate.

It was exactly like the crate he'd lived under in Ayr. Something told him that as impossible as it seemed, this *was* his crate. He'd lived in it for many moons before he was invited to come to Grant land in the Highlands. He glanced over his shoulder, taking in all the familiar surroundings, smells, and sounds, which reminded him of what it had been like to live on the roads of Ayr, hungry and alone and cold.

He'd begged for most of what he ate at the time, though he'd found a nearby inn that used to save scraps for him once the travelers moved on.

The sound of running feet came from behind him.

"Leave off, you surly brute. Those are my belongings you're wantin' to steal."

Loki spun around to see a laddie running toward him, a furious expression on his face. Dark disheveled locks that hadn't seen a comb in days hung to his collar. A dirty face stared up at him with sharp eyes and a fierce scowl, a jutted chin daring Loki to challenge him. He looked to be the same age or just a wee bit younger than Loki had been whilst living in his crate.

"Bugger off, you auld man. Why'd you want my stuff? You'll no' get my crates either. I've taken good care of all three of them."

Loki stared about the area, only then noticing that this lad's home was larger than his own had been. He'd found two more crates and arranged them as additional protection against the approaching cold weather.

"Problem, Loki?" Logan stood at the end of the alley next to the inn, both hands on his hips.

"Nay, no problem, Uncle. I was just leaving." Loki stared at the lad.

"Aye, he was just leaving. So bugger off, auld man." His chin lifted another notch and he gave Loki his most aggressive expression, one he'd clearly practiced well.

Loki recalled how often he'd had to keep others from stealing his goods—his crate, his moth-eaten gloves, the one plaid he'd found for warmth, even the pan on which he'd carved his initials with a dagger. Instinct and memory told him that pan sat directly in front of him.

Loki leaned down and picked up the pan, but not before the urchin took a swing at him with his dagger. Catching the lad's arm just in time, Loki said, "Calm down. I'll not steal it. I'd just like to take a look at it."

"That pan is mine, no' yours. It belonged to somebody special." The lad continued to grab for the pan, but Loki held him at bay. Logan continued to stand there at the end of the alley, watching and listening.

"Aye, it did, lad." He turned the pan over and smiled. There they were, his initials—LL for Lucky Loki.

"How would you know? It belonged to a lad

named Lucky Loki, and those are his initials he carved in it himself. He was so good with a sling, he became a hero in the battle with the Norse at Largs."

Loki smiled and peered down at the lad. "Is that so? How did you hear about Lucky Loki?"

"Everyone knows about Lucky Loki. He's a hero. He fought so hard that Laird Alexander Grant, the Highlander with the horse in chain mail that scart the Norse away, took him to the Highlands to be his son."

"Truly?" Loki could not help but grin. He had a reputation he'd known nothing about. A hero? Had the lad truly called him a hero?

"You canno' have it, 'tis mine. If you try to steal it, I'll hunt you down." The cheeky lad bounced up and down, trying to reach his invaluable pan.

Loki didn't know what to say. Not that long ago, he had stood in this lad's place, hoping every day for some meat and enough rainwater to drink. "I'll not steal it from you, lad." He handed it back to the boy.

"Nay, 'tis valuable and 'tis mine. I'll sell it someday. Mayhap he'll come back."

"Who?"

"Lucky Loki, o' course. Mayhap he'll come back and adopt me."

Loki stared at him in shock. Aye, he should. He should do for this lad just what his uncle had done for him—adopt him and take him back to Grant land. He stared into the hopeful eyes, but it would not do. Not now. He was not in the same place his sire had been.

"We need to move on, lad," Logan yelled.

"Aye," he answered. He then turned his gaze back to the urchin. "I hope you meet Lucky Loki someday."

His eyes lit up. "Or mayhap Laird Alexander Grant will adopt me, too."

"What's your name?" Loki asked.

"Kenzie. Sometimes I call myself Lucky Kenzie, but no one else will. Will ye?"

"Aye, Lucky Kenzie it is. Where are your parents?"

"They both died of the fever, so I came to the burgh."

Loki turned away and headed back to the street, but halfway there, he stopped and glanced over his shoulder. "You're wrong, lad."

"About what?" Kenzie gave him a puzzled look, clearly believing he knew all.

"Alex Grant did not adopt him. His brother Brodie did." He tossed the lad a silver coin, enough to buy him food for a couple of days.

The lad caught it and yelled, "My thanks," his eyes lighting up.

Chapter Six

Loki finally gets a name on his search for his real sire.

Later, once the music got underway, they moved toward the outside of the hall. Just as Loki had predicted, they had only taken two steps into the passageway when high-pitched giggles sounded behind them. Sure enough, Tessa came toward him, her arm intertwined with her friend's.

Loki whirled around and flashed a grin at the

ladies, stopping them both in their tracks. "Evening, Lady Tessa. Have you met my friend, Torrian?"

Tessa gave Torrian a lingering look and then sidled up to him and rubbed her body against his. In a husky voice, just loud enough for Loki to hear, she whispered, "Nay, we have not met, but I'd sure like to get to know him better. This is my friend, Dona."

Loki bowed to Dona. "Good eve to you, lass." Giggling and lowering her dark lashes, she slipped her hand around Loki's elbow.

Tessa grabbed Torrian's arm and said, "Follow me." She led them through the torch-lit maze to a small chamber.

Just as Loki was about to step into the chamber, he recognized the man he'd seen earlier. He was headed directly toward them, so Loki motioned to Torrian. "Go on in, I'll be right there." Loki and Torrian had discussed how to go about ferreting information from the lasses, but he did not trust the man with the eye patch. Addressing Dona, he said, "I'll return in a moment." He hurried down the corridor, but suddenly the man with the patch increased his pace. Loki caught up with him, but the two collided, and the man fell to the floor. He cursed fluently, and when Loki offered him a helping hand, he shrugged it off and headed back toward the great hall.

Loki shouted, "My apologies." Patch man ignored him. Loki's gaze searched his clothing for any indication of who he was or what he was about. Giving up, he hurried back to Dona's side and held the door for her to enter the chamber. Inside, there were two small pallets and a small table surrounded by four chairs in front of the hearth. Goblets of wine sat atop the table. Torrian and Tessa had already started to drink wine.

Tessa said, "This is much better than the ale. You should try it." She glanced at Loki and fluttered her eyelashes, implying that her flirtation with his friend had changed nothing between them.

Loki sat on the corner of the table. "Nay, mayhap in a few minutes. Tell me about Ayr. We have not been here in a while. We're from the Highlands."

"What do you wish to know?" Tessa asked.

"Who's the most powerful man in the area, besides the king?"

"I do not know. Why do you ask?" Tessa answered, a subtle movement in her lower jaw.

Loki was quite sure Tessa did not like the direction of the conversation, but he didn't allow her body language to stop him. If anything, it made him more intrigued. "Is there a certain earl or viscount that is the primary vassal to the king?"

"Alexander of Dundonald is still his favorite, but there are others." Tessa took a sip of her wine, a suspicious look in her eyes.

Loki tired of her game, for he knew it *was* a game. He decided to move things along. "Just wondering who would be powerful enough to steal the king's jewels."

"What do you know about the jewels?" Dona asked, her back straightening.

"I know naught. I heard the missing jewels mentioned in the great hall. As I explained, we just got here from the Highlands. Do you know what happened to them?" Loki caught the glance exchanged by Dona and Tessa, and a sour feeling crept into his gut.

"Nay," Dona replied. "But I'd sure be appreciative of anyone who gave me gemstones like the royal jewels."

Loki tipped his head toward Torrian. "I'll return in a moment. Need the garderobe."

"Again?" Tessa asked.

Loki winked at her, "Aye, I drank quite a bit of ale with my meal. I promise to return post haste." He crept out of the chamber, looking both ways before he stepped into the passageway. His intuition was not telling him anything good. As he made his way to the garderobe, he listened for any strange sounds, checking every nook of the mazelike corridors before making his way back.

When he entered the chamber, the first thing he heard was a gurgling noise.

A bald muscular man was holding a dagger to Torrian's throat.

Loki's gaze searched the room. The two girls stood in opposite corners, as far from the mischief as possible. The man was of rather large proportions, and it was clear he was waiting for Loki to act. There was noticeable sweat across Torrian's brown, but Loki was pleased to see there was also fury there.

Humph. This would be easy.

Loki took a few steps toward his cousin.

"Halt. Do not take another step or your friend dies."

Loki did as he was told and froze in place. "No reason to hurt anyone. What is the problem? Why are you here? We've done naught wrong, we're just two traveling Highlanders looking for some entertainment." He smiled, hoping to give the impression that they were two foolish young lads.

The brute's dark gaze skewered into Loki. "Why are you asking about the jewels?"

Loki shrugged his shoulders. "Because we heard about them and hoped to uncover them and become heroes. No other reason. Why do you not release my friend?"

"I ask the questions, not you." He tightened his hold on Torrian, who turned a darker shade of red. "My assistant will be here soon to tie you up."

"Why must you tie us up? We've done naught wrong. Tessa and Dona promised us a sweet eve of pleasure. 'Tis all we were seeking. Let us go and we'll be on our way." Loki managed to move himself to the exact spot he needed for good aim.

The door opened and the man with the eye patch stepped inside and closed the door behind him.

"Where have you been, Egan?" Clyde asked. "Get control of him. Find your dagger. 'Tis the only way he'll talk."

Egan reached into his hidden belt, but he came out with naught besides a puzzled expression. "Clyde? Where's my…"

"That could be a problem," Loki announced, both hands on his hips.

Clyde smirked, "And why is that?"

Loki winked at him as Egan reached into his boot for another weapon. "Seems I have Egan's weapons." Loki flung one dagger straight into Clyde's thigh, then pulled out a second dagger and twisted Egan around until he had the dagger pressed to the man's throat.

As soon as the dagger was embedded in Clyde's thigh, Torrian swung the man around and pointed his dagger at his throat, though the stronger warrior was a little harder to restrain than Egan had been.

Loki said, "Not bad, cousin. Nice job, especially with one his size. I didn't know you had those kinds of moves." Clyde only growled in response.

Torrian said, "He is my uncle, you'll remember, and he has taught me a few things. How'd you get his weapons?"

Loki laughed. "Didn't trust the fellow, so I knocked him down in the passageway and stole his weapons."

Torrian grinned. "Nice strategy. I have much to learn."

Squeezing the dagger against Egan's throat, Loki said, "Now, would you mind telling us what you know about the missing jewels and why you're after us?"

Neither Egan nor Clyde responded. Loki squeezed again.

"All right, I'll tell," Egan spewed. "And this has naught to do with the missing jewels."

"You wee fool! Blackett will whip you."

"I do not care, Clyde. I've had enough. We have naught to do with the jewels. We've been hired by another to follow you both."

Loki squeezed again.

"Nay! I'll talk…"

Loki gave him a moment to catch his breath before squeezing again.

"Are you not Loki Grant of the Highlands?"

"Who wants to know?" Loki ground out.

"Your father," Egan spit out. "The Earl of Cliffnock is your sire."

Chapter Sixteen

Loki finally remembers…

Loki jerked up in his pallet, panting. His gaze searched the room, but there was nothing amiss. The rest of the guards were sleeping. Finally, the memories settled in. He had been dreaming… again…another horrific dream of his childhood. He rubbed his face to try to erase the awful sensations coursing through his body, but they did not fade so easily.

After grabbing his plaid, his sword, and his boots, he headed outside. He paced in circles under the starless night and then made his way over to the loch. Standing there, he stared down at the glassy surface as if something could rise out of the cold water and tell him he had imagined every bit of it.

But it didn't happen. This was the third night in a row that memories of his life as a wee one had kept him awake. One night he had dreamed of his mother, another night about his father. But this night's dream had been the worst…

Hamish. He'd dreamed of Hamish. He sat down on a cold rock and relived all that he'd just experienced. There was no choice but to suffer through it again, for he believed it was all true.

This dream had been different from the others. While the dreams of his mother had been fleeting images and thoughts, sometimes just a smell, the nightmare of Hamish had been as detailed as if he had lived it.

He was quite sure he had. He'd just discovered why he could not recall how he had made it to Ayr.

The nightmare began in a small hut. The cottage had two rooms in it, and he was alone in one with Hamish. He could hear his father yelling at his fair-haired mother, but the only thing he recalled about his mother was that she was sobbing and saying "Please, Edward" over and over again.

He had no idea what she wanted, and he could not recall anything his father said, but what he did remember was that he ran through the door and told his father to stay away from his mother.

His father punched him in the face, his mother cried out, "Nay, Edward!", and the next memory he had was riding in a cart. He woke up under a large blanket, the wheels of the cart hitting rocks and stones, bouncing him up and down. He peeked out from beneath the blanket to see where he was going. Hamish was riding the horse that pulled the cart, and he could see the moon overhead, the stars twinkling in the dead of night. When the cart finally stopped, he sat up and uncovered himself, only realizing his eye was swollen after he tried to brush the sleep from them. Poking his face in other spots, he realized his father's fist had bruised him this time.

This time. Loki put his face in his hands trying to grapple with his thoughts. Had his father beaten him frequently at a young age? Never had Brodie Grant once raised a hand to him, and his uncles had never beaten their bairns either.

Loki forced himself to recall the details from the rest of the dream.

Hamish had pulled the horse into a clearing in the woods. After dismounting, he stalked to the back of the cart, grabbed Loki by the neck, and hoisted him out of the cart.

"Finally, I'll do what I've always wanted to do with you, you wee wise arse."

Loki didn't say a word, but just stared at this man he hated.

"Your sire has finally had enough of your wise remarks and told me to do as I please with you." He grinned at him. "You opened your mouth a few too many times, and you think you're smarter that everyone else, do you not?"

Loki couldn't help himself. He knew he shouldn't say aught, but for some reason, he wanted the last word with this cruel man.

"'Tis not hard being smarter than you, you piece of shite."

It felt good to curse this man—so good that he smiled. He saw a familiar look in Hamish's eyes—the blind fury that usually preceded his fist. The big man lifted Loki out of the cart and pummeled him, throwing him a good distance through the air. When he landed, Hamish stalked to his side, leaned over him, and whispered, "Your sire never wants to see you again, so I thought I'd enjoy taking your last breath, lad, but instead I'd rather have the animals feed on you."

Then he strode away and left him there to die.

Aye, this dream was real—he knew it without a doubt. Tears streamed down his face. The memories were brutal, but it explained why Hamish and the earl had treated him so horribly. They'd always hated him, apparently threatened by the acuity of his mind. His own father had sent him off with a brute, and the brute had left him to die. For some unknown reason, his mind had protected itself from the painful memory for years.

After he brushed the tears from his face, he did the only thing he could do. He raced to the keep and made his way to his parents' chamber. He sneaked inside, not wanting to wake his brother and sisters, for he had to see his Bella.

Chapter Twenty

Loki goes back for Kenzie and invites him to join Clan Grant.

Moving back through Doongait and on to Woodgait, Loki slowed his horse. Brodie gave him a look of curiosity, which was not a surprise—Loki had not told him aught about Kenzie. As soon as he neared the inn, he shouted, "Kenzie!"

The young lad shot out from behind the building, his eyes alight with excitement. "You came back for me?"

A surprised look filled Brodie's face, followed by a small grin as he took in the young lad in front of him. Loki wondered if his sire remembered this spot.

Loki replied, "I did come back for you. Kenzie, this is my sire, Brodie Grant."

Brodie gave each of them a weighing look. "Seems I've seen someone like this before," he finally said.

Kenzie jumped up and down. "Aye, I live where Lucky Loki lived, so someday I'll be lucky, too."

Brodie returned his gaze to his son, curious to see what would happen next.

"Kenzie, have you seen the wee lass you found before?"

"Bella? Aye, Blackett's men have her at the castle," he said with a scowl. "I tried to tell the sheriff, but he would not listen to me. She could be hurt. I don't like the earl. He and his men are mean. And I can help you find her. I sneaked behind them one day, so I saw where the secret tunnel to the castle is hidden."

Loki's mouth curved, for this was just the discovery he'd been hoping to make. "How do you know she's there?"

"Because Blackett's second came through to hire a bunch of men to guard his castle. He also hired the best archer in England to kill someone. Never said who, but they say he's the best." His nose scrunched up. "I heard Ramsay's wife is the best of the Scots."

"You heard right, now continue. What else did you hear about Blackett?"

"The second said Blackett would be attacked soon and he needed help. He promised a lot of coin, so some Lowlanders went with him. But some that left came back. I overheard them talking. They said Blackett was holding someone's wife at his keep, and he would bring all the Highlands down on them. 'Tis why they left. They did not wish to fight the savage Highlanders from way up north. Are you a savage? You do not look like a savage." He peered at them with such a serious expression it almost made Loki choke.

Holding a hand down to the laddie, Loki said, "Do you wish to travel with me? I'm not riding in to an easy situation, but I could use your help. We are always looking for someone who can uncover information for us without raising suspicion." He wouldn't discuss it with his sire now, but Kenzie was going home with him to Grant land. He could live with him and Bella, or wherever he wished to live. They'd make it work somehow. He couldn't desert the lad again, not when the cold winter was about to bear down on him.

Brodie cocked his brow at Loki. "Like you did with me," Loki glanced at his sire, speaking only loud enough for him to hear.

Brodie nodded. "Suits me if it suits you. He seems like a resourceful lad."

"I'm coming," Kenzie yelled out, "but let me hide some things first so no one steals from me." He tore back behind the building, and Loki saw him dash into the trees.

Loki waited until the laddie was out of hearing distance, then explained to his sire. "He found Bella when she was about to fall from her horse from cold and exhaustion. He wrapped her in plaids, then moved her in the back before he came to find me."

Brodie nodded. "That explains everything."

Loki hung his head as he whispered, "He also found a pan with the initials 'LL' inscribed with a knife in the middle of the bottom."

Kenzie raced toward them, only a plaid in his hand.

"Do you have anything else of importance, lad?" Brodie asked, an unreadable expression on his face.

The laddie gazed up at Brodie Grant, hesitant to answer for some reason. "Aye, my lord."

"What is it?" Brodie asked, in a quiet yet stern voice with which Loki was quite familiar.

"Uhhh…"

"Speak up, lad."

Kenzie swallowed and said, "My mama sewed me a fabric puppy before she died."

"Then you better get something that important. We won't be coming back."

"Aye, my lord." Kenzie hurried through the walkway and returned with his well-worn puppy. "Where am I going, my lord?"

"Home," Brodie replied. "'Tis time for you to go home with us after we're done with this wee skirmish."

Kenzie's face lit up as he stared at Loki in delight.

Loki gave his father an appreciative look and then held his hand down to the laddie. "Aye, you're moving in with the Grants. Welcome to the clan."

Chapter Twenty-One

Loki meets the "rat bastard" again.

He walked toward the gate, his gaze searching for any sign of Bella. He noticed the area around the keep was quite empty—the clan members he'd seen here on his first visit had apparently deserted the earl. He was told to wait outside the gate for the earl to come to him.

That's when his world collapsed. The Earl of Cliffnock lumbered toward him, his hand holding a dagger to the delicate throat of his wife. Loki had no moves. Alex had told him not to worry, that the situation would be handled from inside. When activity exploded in the keep, Alex and his men would be ready to attack. But there was no sign of Kenzie or the others.

What if Kenzie had failed?

"Set the bag down, but don't come any closer. I want it on that tree stump over there. I'll not play the fool again, Loki." The earl's eyes danced with a look of superiority.

Hamish came out from behind him. "No wise arse remarks today, Loki? Are you sure you do not wish to take me on? One wee fight. Whoever brings the first to the ground wins. What do you say? The earl gave me permission to fight you, just once."

Loki stood, his gaze not moving from the earl's. "Here's your coin. Release my wife—we have an agreement." He placed the sack on the tree stump Blackett had indicated, his gaze locked on the dagger at Bella's throat.

Hamish continued to throw his best taunts his way, but he would not allow the brutish man to distract him from his focus.

His father said, "I do have an agreement with Hamish. He wants a fight with you. I'm of a mind to allow it. What say you, son?"

"I'm not your son, and I am naught like you. Free Bella as you promised. I am not interested in battling with Hamish. I only want my wife."

The grin that exploded on Edward Blackett's face told Loki the man had known all along that he was not his sire.

"Nay, 'tis true, you're not really mine. You are too much of a lass like your mother."

Loki ignored the laughter from the opposing guards, his gaze still fixed on Bella.

Then the only thing that could sway his mind happened.

Hamish reached over and rubbed Bella's bottom, and she chirped, a sound that traveled straight to his soul in an instant.

Chapter Twenty-Two

Loki would kill the rat bastard for touching his Bella. A loud growl erupted from him and he dove at Hamish, throwing three punches at the man's face before he could react. Hamish swung his leg out, catching the back of Loki's knees and dropping him to the ground with a roar. He punched Loki in the belly twice before he was able to roll away.

Blood ran down Hamish's face, and to Loki's disgust, the animal actually licked it and smirked as he hopped back onto his feet. The two circled one another, Hamish taunting Loki, Loki refusing to respond. Taking the older man totally by surprise, Loki flipped onto his hands and hit him hard in the chest with both feet before he landed upright again. He then pounced on him and pummeled his face. After throwing two punches to the man's belly, Loki grabbed him by the throat, swearing to choke the life out of him. Just then, Hamish kicked him square in the ballocks, bringing him to his knees. Hamish had to fight to get back to his feet, gagging to regain his wind, while Loki fought the sheer pain of the blow. Just as he made it to his feet again, Hector tossed his sword at Hamish.

"A sword against an unarmed man? Fair contest, aye?" Loki blew the hair out of his eyes and fought to level his breathing, reminding himself that being in control was more important than having the most powerful weapon. His sire and his uncle had taught him well, and he would be victorious. Uncle Alex had often told him that all his training could ultimately be for only one fight, but that fight would mean life or death for him or a loved one. How true his words were.

Hamish swung the sword over his head and heaved it toward Loki's middle, but he easily spun away, causing the older man to stumble. Taking several steps away, Loki tried to come up with a plan to best the sword. But there was no need. Logan appeared behind him on his horse and tossed him a sword.

Satisfaction crossed his face as the cold hard hilt of the sword rubbed against the calluses of his hands. This was his sword—the sword crafted by Brodie Grant for his son. He swung the weapon a couple of times away from Hamish to get the feel of it again, then he waited for the lout to move toward him. Patience, Uncle Alex had often told him—patience, skill, and brute strength would always win the day.

Hamish moved his one hand, a move Loki had been trained to watch for, something that meant a warrior was about to switch his grip. At the exact moment when Hamish changed hands, Loki swung his sword in a wide arc, a move he'd practiced many times. But this time was different, for this time his swing was fueled with hatred for the man who'd mistreated his mother and with fury for the man who'd dared touch his wife.

Throwing his entire body behind the force of the arc, he caught Hamish in the arm first, causing blood to shoot up from his body, then buried the sword deep into his belly.

Hamish's eyes turned dull as he crumpled to the ground, clutching for something—anything—to avoid the fate he'd sought. Instead, the life force drained from every part of him. "Wise-arse bastard."

Loki grabbed the hilt of the sword and twisted it, forcing an eerie sound from Hamish's throat. "Rat bastard. This is from the wee lad you left in the forest alone to die."

He turned to the earl and whispered, "Let. Her. Go."

The earl shoved Bella toward Loki, grabbed the coin, and raced back toward the portcullis.

He ran toward the gate screaming, "Close the gate once I'm in and the archer is out!"

Chapter Twenty-Three

Loki meets his real father.

Kenzie skipped along behind Loki and Bella, firing questions too fast for Loki to answer. "So is the Grant castle as big as they say? Do you think they'll allow me to stay? Mayhap I could find a job to do…I know! I could be a stable lad, and I promise to work verra hard."

Loki grinned and continued over to their horses, casting a sly grin at Bella, who was clearly as amused as he was by Kenzie's exuberance.

"Oh, wait! Loki. Did you say during supper that you wish to marry your wife again? There's a nice priest here who would love to marry you proper. He's a Blackfriar at the kirk on the other side of town, but I like him."

"Bella and I are married proper, lad. I just mentioned that mayhap we would have a celebration back in the Grant hall someday. We do not need to be married again." He leaned over and kissed Bella's cheek before he helped her to mount her horse.

"But you really would like Father Prestwick."

He scurried over next to Loki, peering up at him with such hope in his face, it took him back a few decades. He remembered feeling the exact same way about Brodie Grant. "Kenzie," he said as gently as he could, "we really do not have much extra time. Winter is coming to the Highlands soon, and 'twill be a harsh enough trip as it is. If we delay any longer, it could be disastrous." Loki lifted Kenzie up in front of Bella. That was a mistake, because now Kenzie could look at him eye-to-eye.

"Please, Loki. Father is the only one I need to say goodbye to. He's the only one who would wonder what became of me. He gave me food many times and let me sleep in his kirk when the coldest nights fell in winter."

He couldn't deny the look in the lad's eyes, so he peeked at Bella, who gave him a slight nod.

"I promise 'twill be quick."

Loki spun around and mounted his horse. "All right, lad, but only for a few moments." He motioned to their guards to follow.

Kenzie's face lit up and he clapped his hands. "You'll no' regret it."

"Lead the way." Loki tipped his head in the direction of the kirk, wondering when he'd turned into such a soft-hearted fool.

Once they reached the kirk, Kenzie jumped down and ran over to Loki's horse, tugging on his hand. "Come along, I promise you'll love Father Prestwick."

"Bella and I will wait outside. You run in and give Father a hug."

"Nay—" Kenzie's face fell, "—I want you to meet him. 'Twill only take a moment. Please?"

Loki sighed and slid off his horse, then wrapped his hands around his wife's waist and helped her dismount. "Bella, let's go inside and warm up for a bit." He turned to the guards, "We'll return shortly."

Kenzie pushed the door open and ran down the aisle, calling for the priest all the while. Loki and Bella followed him inside. The kirk was remarkable, and the tapestries and woodworking were some of the most beautiful Loki had ever seen. The altar had red cloths trimmed in gold threads, covered kneelers, and thick pillows with carefully tended needlework on each one. The lad disappeared through a door to fetch the priest, presumably in the Blackfriar living quarters behind the altar.

A few moments later, Kenzie came through the door tugging on the hand of the priest, a tall man with brown hair peppered with streaks of silver. He had a kind smile, and when he finally managed to pull away from the wee lad, he bowed to them, his hands clasped together at his waist. He stood in front of the altar, a distance away from them yet.

"Greetings and welcome to the House of Our Lord. I am Father Francis Prestwick, and I'm pleased to hear you will be taking Kenzie to your home. He is a good, hard-working soul, whom I will miss dearly. He reminds me of my own son."

Loki and Bella stayed at the back of the building, Bella seated and Loki standing next to her, his hand on her shoulder. "We promise to take good care of him, Father."

"The lad tells me you are Loki Grant of the legend of the Norse battle?"

"Legend? I'm not sure about that, Father, but aye, I am Loki Grant and this is my wife Bella." Loki took a few steps in the direction of the friar.

Kenzie bolted down the aisle and yanked on Loki's hand. "Come closer, you must see Father Prestwick closer."

His mischievous grin made Loki pause—the lad was clearly up to something—but he decided to venture closer to the priest anyway. Loki had to admit the man had a certain pull to him. He moved down the center of the aisle, Bella following directly behind him.

As he approached the priest, Loki dipped his head, then lifted his eyes to meet the other man's gaze. Bella gasped behind him and wee Kenzie was practically dancing on his feet behind the priest, a wide grin on his face. "Do you see what I see, Loki?"

Aye, he did. The priest's eyes widened as he stared at Loki. "Are you the son of Ciara Blackett?" he choked out.

Loki nodded, unable to speak for a moment. The priest had one blue eye and one green eye, just as he did. Loki glanced at Kenzie and whispered, "You knew."

Kenzie nodded, a grin still on his face. "You are the only two I ever met with eyes of different colors, and yet they are exactly the same. Do you no' think 'tis odd? You would no' have believed me if I told you. You had to see for yourself."

A fine tremor shook the priest's hands as he whispered, "Excuse me, I think I need to sit down for a moment."

Loki helped him to a nearby bench, then sat down beside him. "Are you all right, Father?"

"Aye. If you'll give me a moment to collect myself, I'd be happy to explain." He reached inside his robe and pulled out a linen square, wiping his forehead and his cheeks before he set it back inside his robe. "Kenzie, would you do me the favor of taking Bella into my chambers? You can find a piece of fruit for each of you."

"Aye, Father." Kenzie held his hand out to Bella, who leaned down to kiss Loki's cheek before she left.

Chapter Twenty-Three

Loki is finally able to say the words in his heart to his parents.

Brodie made his way over to Bella, and Loki could see his mother's gaze on him, her happiness and unconditional love washing over him like the softest of furs. He stood by the door like a statue.

He didn't know how. Hellfire, he had been so certain he would finally be able to tell her how he felt. He'd rehearsed it over and over in his mind on their trek.

Bella, Celestina, and Brodie chatted as he leaned against the door, attempting to organize his thoughts, failing miserably as comment after comment brewed in his mind only to be tossed aside as insufficient.

How did one do it?

How did one person thank another for taking him from squalor? For renewing his hope and faith? At the age of seven or eight summers, he had feared he would be forever cold, forever hungry, forever lonely…nay…forever alone. Instead, Brodie and Celestina Grant had made him forever loved, forever grateful, and forever happy and full of life.

"Loki?" It was his mother's voice, the sweet cadence that was a comfort to his soul. "Are you all right?"

"Mama, I just wanted…I would like…" The words just wouldn't come.

His sire wrapped his arm around his mother's waist. "Son?"

He tried again, forcing the words beyond the lump in his throat, "I met my true sire. He's a Blackfriar, a nice man. I'll tell you about him sometime. But I just wanted to tell you…"

He saw the quick twinge of disappointment in their eyes before they masked it. Och, how he hated to cause them pain. Then he knew. No more. It was in his power to comfort his mother, and he would do it.

Bella stood off to the corner, his beautiful Bella,

and as if she could read the words in his heart, she gave him a slight nod of encouragement.

"I just wanted to tell you that I appreciate all you've done for me, loving me the way you have—" he paused for long enough to see the delight emerge in his mother's eyes, "—and that you will always be my true parents. You took me in when I needed it most, and you've been wonderful every day since then, and I will be forever grateful…forever."

His mother ambled toward him, her steps shaky and graceless, which was completely out of character for her. She'd always waited for him to come to her. "Oh, Loki. You know we love you, and I'd be overjoyed to hear about your true sire." She reached up to wrap her arms around him at the same time that his father grasped his shoulder.

His mouth opened, and the words he uttered were weak, but audible nonetheless. "I love you both."

"Loki, did something happen we are not aware of?" Brodie asked.

"Nay, I just…it took me a long time to believe I deserved to come here, but now I do. And I understand what was in your hearts when you took me in."

"Do you?" His mother cupped his cheeks to bring his gaze down to hers. "Do you understand what it was like for me to be locked in a chamber for most of my life, with no friends or family who loved me?"

His head ached terribly from the truth of her words. "Aye, I do."

"That is correct, you do. And you and your father helped to put an end to that for me. So you are more than deserving of the good will that has come your way since then. Please do not ever forget that. You found a way into our hearts quickly. But you seem to understand that a bit better now."

Loki's knees threatened to buckle, but the booming sound of his father's voice forced them back to a locked position. "Let's get something to eat and let Kenzie know we have not deserted him. Celestina, wait until you meet this new lad."

Finally, the strings that had been choking his soul loosened, freeing him from all the things that had been niggling at him for quite some time.

Chapter Twenty-Four

Loki is granted Castle Curanta as its chieftain, and he and Bella adopt Kenzie.

After they had all stuffed themselves, Alex stood at the dais, his usual movement when he was about to make a speech. The large crowd settled quickly.

"As most of you are aware, our clan was once again challenged by an evil force that attempted to hurt one of our own and steal some of our wealth. We were able to easily put an end to this threat. I thank all the warriors for traveling with me, as well as their wives for supporting them in this venture.

"Fortunately, the battle was short. Loki, Bella, and Kenzie, come forward please."

Kenzie's eyes bulged, but he came forward as requested, his wee legs trembling, bending his neck as far back as he could to gaze up at Alex Grant. Bella reached down to squeeze his hand in a show of support.

"I cannot tell you how proud I am of my nephew, Loki Grant," Alex continued, "who demonstrated the value of his years of hard work and training in front of all of us. He fought hard and achieved a quick victory in a pivotal sword fight. I also wish to commend Kenzie, who helped us from start to finish, and was the person who retrieved King Alexander's jewels."

Shouts and cheers erupted from the clan, and Kenzie beamed from all the attention.

Alex raised his hands to quiet everyone. "Kenzie, we are pleased to have you at Clan Grant, and there are two people here who are interested in adopting you if you agree. Loki and Bella would like you to be their son if you are agreeable."

Kenzie's delight and surprise told them all how he felt. He burst into tears and looked from Bella to Loki, then back again. He ran to Bella and hugged her tight, then rushed over to Loki to do the same. He stared at both of them with a tear-stained face and asked, "I do not have to live alone? I have parents and a Mama and a Papa again?"

Bella knelt in front of him, Loki right beside her, and the sight of the lad's crumpled face nearly broke her heart. She couldn't imagine what Loki must be thinking and wondered how close this was to his life. "Aye, 'tis true, Kenzie, if you wish to stay with us."

"Aye, I prayed every day, just like Father Brian and Father Francis told me. I asked for a new mama and papa, and now you are here." He hugged them again. "Many thanks. I love you both."

Bella's tears slid down her cheeks, but she wiped them away when Alex motioned for them to stand.

"This really is not finished yet, though I'm pleased to see that Kenzie Grant will officially be your son. We have taken over a small castle not far from here, and my brothers and I have decided that we wish to ask Loki to take over as chieftain of the keep."

Gasps of surprise and cheers and whistles greeted Alex's announcement. Bella's heart swelled with pride as she turned to look at Loki. He met her gaze with a question in his eyes. "What do you think?"

Bella nodded with tears in her eyes. "Aye. I'll go anywhere you wish to go, Loki. Forever."

Epilogue

Welcome, Lucas!

Bella stepped cautiously, her hands on Maddie's shoulder, making her way from the chair back to the changed bed.

"There you are," Maddie said. "Do you not feel much better with a fresh gown on? We'll get you back in bed so you can rest. What a fine son you have."

"Many thanks, Lady Madeline."

"Once we get you settled, I'll get Loki to bring the bairn back up to you. Have you decided what you'd like to name him?"

Bella frowned as she thought back on all the names she and Loki had discussed. "We tried many times, but we just could not come up with the perfect name without having first seen the babe. Once he returns, we'll discuss it."

Once they had her in bed and covered with furs again, a knock sounded on the door. Loki entered carrying their bairn with Father Prestwick, Celestina, and Brodie trailing behind them. Caralyn motioned to Ashlyn and Maddie, and they all stepped out of the chamber to make room for the others.

"Good eve to you, my lady," Father Prestwick said.

"Father? What a lovely surprise." Bella glanced at her husband to see his reaction, but he seemed pleased. Brodie and Celestina both had genuine smiles on their faces, so she hoped Father Prestwick's visit was acceptable to all.

"I apologize for the surprise at such a moment. I had no idea, but I confess that I am overjoyed to see the babe."

Celestina pulled a stool out for him. "Father, please sit." She sat in the chair next to him. "Bella, we're all pleased to meet Father Prestwick, and he wished to give you his best wishes. I promise we will not tire you."

"Aye, congratulations on your new bairn." Brodie kissed her cheek.

"Father? Would you mind giving a wee blessing on our son?"

"Why, of course, lass. I'd be delighted."

He took his place beside Loki and reached for the babe's forehead, but then stopped. "What's his name?"

He glanced at Loki, then at Bella, but neither spoke. Bella nodded at Loki, because she knew her husband and could see in his gaze that he had thought of the perfect name.

He leaned down to kiss her cheek, then gazed at the beautiful babe in his arms.

"Lucas. His name is Lucas."

Torrian

Book 2

Torrian and Loki became close, being a bit older than many in the second generation.

CHAPTER TWENTY-ONE

Loki meets his sister, Heather.

TWO DAYS LATER, they had not gotten much further in their planning and they slept apart, though Torrian loved to sneak kisses from her. He'd told her they would marry when he'd return, but each time she'd mentioned their wedding, he'd changed the subject. She did not understand why, but she believed the wedding had taken on some form of secrecy. Her only concern was marrying in front of a crowd. She was definitely more comfortable around his family, but would she be able to marry him in front of his entire clan?

Some of the Grants arrived that day, though she was unsure if it was expected or not, but she was too busy trying to sew herself a new gown for her wedding to pay much attention. The garment was a pale green color similar to the buds on the trees in early spring. Nellie was off with her new friends. A knock sounded at her door, and she beckoned the caller inside.

Brenna stood in her doorway. "If you are not too busy, lass, we'd like to invite you to a special gathering."

Heather had no idea what Brenna was about, but

she adored her mother-to-be and would never turn her down. Having never had a mother or father, she treasured Torrian's parents and hoped to have a strong relationship with them. So far, they had been wonderful. "Of course," she said.

Though she followed Brenna down the passageway without question, she could not imagine where she was being led or why. There were many Grants chatting in the great hall, but Brenna led her past them, to where Torrian was standing beside the door to his sire's solar. He held his hand out to her, and she gladly took it. She wished to ask him what to expect, but she found she could not.

Brenna kissed her on the cheek and walked away, which puzzled her even more. "I know this will be a shock to you," Torrian said, reaching up to stroke her face, "but I think you'll be pleased."

He must have seen the confusion on her face because he kissed her cheek and said, "Trust me, lass. I have chosen to do this in this manner because I love you so."

With a sudden whoosh inside her belly, her fear took over.

She clutched his hand with a death grip, and she could feel her heartbeat speed up. Glancing at him, she tried to speak but naught came out. The laughter of the group echoed behind her, reminding her how many were now in the hall. Could she handle this?

Torrian stopped, placed his finger under her chin, and locked his gaze on hers. "Sweeting, 'twill be all right. I'm with you. Trust in me."

The entire hall seemed to close in on her as her breathing increased. How would she ever learn to get past her fears? She closed her eyes for a moment to breathe in Torrian's scent in an attempt to relax her body.

"Aye, take another deep breath. I'll not leave your side. Do you trust me?"

She nodded, opening her eyes again slowly, focusing on him.

"Follow me. There are not many inside."

Heather stepped cautiously inside the solar. Father Rab was facing her, talking with another priest who had his back to her. Wee Kenzie was there too, along with another lad speaking to Quade and Brodie.

She took another deep breath and was pleased to feel her insides calm.

Kenzie ran to her side and tugged on her arm. "Please come closer."

He pulled her over to the lad with the tousled, sun-colored hair, and the lad turned to her. At the same time, the priest who was with Father Rab gave her his full attention.

"Heather, this is my adopted cousin, Loki," Torrian said, "and this is his sire, Father Francis Prestwick."

"Greetings," Heather did a small curtsy, but she froze the instant she lifted her gaze to the two in front of her.

Looking at the lad called Loki was like seeing her reflection in the loch, only he was male. She stood a distance away yet, but the pressure of a small pair of hands against her back propelled her forward until she stood almost nose-to-nose with Loki.

A giggle erupted behind her and Kenzie said, "Look closer, lass." Kenzie moved to her side and held his head tilted as if waiting for something.

Then she understood. She stared into Loki's one blue eye and one green eye, and her heart burst open. Then she glanced at his sire, only to gasp again and take a step back.

Torrian squeezed her hand and pulled her to a nearby chair. "I think we should all sit."

Loki took the chair opposite Heather and his sire—could he be *their* sire?—sat next to him. She heard Quade leave the room, and Brodie followed, tugging wee Kenzie by the hand. "You've seen your favorite part, Kenzie."

"I ken, but 'twas it not the best, grandsire? It gets better each time."

Soon the only ones left in the room with her besides Torrian were Loki and the two priests.

Her voice cracked and she whispered, "I do not understand."

"Please, allow me to explain," Father Francis said.

She nodded and folded her hands into her lap while Torrian sat in the chair next to hers and wrapped an arm around her shoulder.

Father Francis said, "Many years ago, I fell in love with the sweetest woman in the world, and I believe she is your mother."

Heather tried to stop her breath from hitching, but she could not.

"Your mother, Ciara Blackett, was married to an evil man. A long time before I became a priest, I lived in a cottage not far from her. I fell in love with your mother, and I am ashamed to say we committed a grave sin. You see, Ciara had two children, Loki, who sits in front of you, and a daughter. I believe both children were mine rather than Blackett's.

This daughter was never named, and I was told that both Ciara and her two children died soon after the daughter's birth. I never met you, but I had seen Loki. I know 'tis possible that I'm wrong and you are not my daughter, but your eye color tells me you are."

Heather looked back and forth between the two men in front of her. Could it be true? Her vision flooded with tears as she stared at these men whose eye coloring was identical to hers.

"It must be true," she whispered. "I've not seen another with eyes like ours."

Father said, "Nay, 'tis quite rare."

She turned to Torrian. "You knew?"

"Aye. I suspected many moons ago when I came upon you while I was in the woods with my pups, but you ran away. At the time, I'd just learned that Loki's sire was alive."

Loki added, "Do not fault Torrian. When he told me about you, I asked him not to share the truth with you. I think 'tis something that must be done in person." Then Loki asked, "Would you mind telling us what you know of your parents? Who raised you? That may help us piece everything together."

Heather stuttered, but she continued. "I was raised by my grandparents in Perthshire, not far from the Buchan land. They told me my mother died in childbirth. I recall meeting an aunt on a couple of occasions, but she was a distance away."

"Do you remember aught about a brother?" Loki's gaze settled on her, unwavering.

Tears misted in her eyes as she thought back to

a day when she was young. Her grandmama had told her she looked like her brother. "Aye, on one occasion my grandmother mentioned a brother, but my grandsire yelled at her." She stared at her hands in her lap. "They never said another word about a brother. I thought she was mistaken. I had no idea…"

Loki said, "I know exactly how you feel, lass. Kenzie brought me to Father Francis the same way."

Tears spilled over onto her cheeks and she reached for Torrian's hand. "I recall one other thing."

Father Francis whispered, "What is it, lass?"

"The only thing they said about my sire was that they hated him. They said my mother was the sweetest creature ever, and my father was cruel."

"Mayhap we should leave it to you, Heather. I cannot prove you are my daughter, but I can attest that your mother was indeed the sweetest creature ever, and if you believe me to be your sire, I'd be happy to tell you all I know about her."

Heather sobbed into her hands, then stood and leaned toward Loki. Wrapping her arms around him, she said, "I'm so happy to meet you, brother." She turned to Father Francis and fell into his arms sobbing. "Will you tell me about my mother someday?"

"Aye, naught would give me more pleasure."

Loki let out a deep breath. "I believe you're my sister. My mother hated Blackett. I've met him and they had good reason to hate him. He beat her. You were fortunate your…our grandparents took you away. I wish I had known them. You have much to share with me."

She turned to him with a questioning look. "You did not know them?"

"Blackett left me to die in the woods after our mother died. I suffered a head injury that took my memories of my life before that. Though some memories have returned, I have none of grandparents. I may have known them, but I do not recall. I lived on the roads of Ayr for years until I was adopted by the Grants. Father Francis is my true sire, but Brodie Grant is my adopted sire."

"Welcome to the family, Heather Preston," Father Francis said. "I must confess, I am the one who asked Father Rab not to marry you until we met. It was too late for me to marry my son and his wife, but I hoped for the opportunity to be the one to marry you and Torrian, if it proved true that you are my daughter."

"I would be honored to have you marry us, Father." Heather laughed and hugged them both. She turned back to gaze at Torrian. "Do you not agree?"

He rubbed his hand in small circles on her back. "Aye. I would be honored, and it pleases me that your brother is my cousin. I hope you are not angry at me for keeping the secret."

She threw her arms around her husband-to-be. "Nay." She paused to give him a thoughtful look, taking in the kindness and love she saw in his gaze. "I do not think I could ever get angry with you."

Loki added, "I heard my sister say that, cousin." He winked at him. "See if she says the same after you've been married for a few moons."

Chapter Twenty-Two

Heather is kidnapped.

Torrian slowed his horse as Loki drew up beside him, and Jake fell in directly behind them.

"You know where they are headed?" Loki asked.

"Not for certes, but there is a deserted hut not far from here. My guess is that's where he's taking her. He has four guards with him."

Jake said, "He'll post the four guards outside while he takes her inside."

Torrian's jaw clenched. He did not want to think about that, but Jake's assessment made sense.

"Who is it?" asked Kenzie. "Who stole her? Ranulf, the whoreson?"

Torrian replied, "'Tis not Ranulf. I saw him fighting at the rear of his warriors." He wasn't ready to reveal the name of Nellie's sire and his suspicions just yet.

Loki snorted. "Somehow, 'tis not a surprise that he hides in the back."

"How should we handle this?" Torrian asked. Loki was well-known for his scheming and trickery while Jake had the most experience in battle since his sire was the infamous Alexander Grant. They would surely know better than he did.

"Your lead. 'Tis your wife," Loki said. "Trust me, when you see her in his hands, your fury will take over. I know."

Torrian recognized the truth in his statement. "We'll take the four guards out first. What's your choice of weapons?"

"Put Kenzie and me in the trees," Loki said. "We'll

play with them a bit first. They won't even know what hit them before 'tis too late."

Kenzie giggled. "Aye, my sire taught me how to be really good with my sling, just like he was." He patted Loki's arm.

Jake nodded. "You hide in the trees, and Torrian and I will wait in the bushes until you get rid of two of them. Then we can take out the other two."

A slow smile crept across Loki's face. "Then whoever has your wife is all yours, cousin."

"Just do not be too slow with this. I do not want him touching her."

"Haste will get a knife in your belly, cousin. Be wise," Jake added.

When they got close, they tied up their horses and crept toward the hut. The four guards were outside just as they expected. Jake found a spot to hide and pointed to a place where Torrian could take cover closer to the hut. Loki lifted Kenzie into a tree the perfect distance to shoot from, then found his own tree to climb.

He winked at Torrian just before he climbed his tree. "Do not worry, cuz. We'll get her back."

Chapter Twenty-Three

Loki and Kenzie at their best.

Torrian watched as Loki wove his own special brand of magic, but this time with a co-conspirator, Kenzie. He heard voices from inside the cottage, but no words were audible. Oh, how he longed to see her.

The door opened and Dugald stepped out,

addressing one of his guards before heading back inside. He dropped the bar in place loud enough to echo across the area.

Torrian ran his hand down his face. Somehow, seeing Dugald in front of him made it worse. He'd kill the whoreson with his bare hands. The only thing that kept him from running inside that very moment was the knowledge that Heather was in that bastard's hands. He could do nothing that would endanger her.

"Ow!" Torrian heard the guard on the opposite side of the field slap his face. "Ian, what the hell did you throw at me? That hurt."

The guard closest to Torrian turned to face the fool. "I did not throw aught. Stop your crying and pay attention."

They settled again at their posts, their eyes fixed on the surrounding area. Another loud bellow sounded from a different guard. "Hell. What in blazes was that, Ian? Are you throwing stones or something? You hit me in my forehead. I'll beat the shite out of you if you do it again."

"What?" Ian said, sounding both defensive and confused. "I did not throw aught."

Another shout followed. "Ow." The fourth guard's hand went to the back of his head. "Ian, you son of a bitch. Do that again and I'll kill you."

Torrian held his laughter in check. Loki and Kenzie were having their fun. Still, he was fast losing his patience, and he wished they would speed things up. His wee wife was inside that cottage with an addled fool.

As if they'd heard his thoughts, several stones

launched at the same time, hitting all four guards enough for them to start hurling insults at Ian. All three charged the beleaguered guard.

Loki jumped out of the tree and landed on one of the guards, cutting his throat in an instant. Kenzie threw another rock that hit the second guard in the temple, knocking him out. Now the numbers were in their favor. Torrian lunged for Ian, the closest to him, dodging two of his thrusts before delivering a jarring blow to the man's midsection, enough to fell him so Loki could finish it.

Jake took care of the fourth guard as a lass's screams rent the air.

Heather.

Torrian raced to the door and did his best to kick it open, but it was well barred. Loki joined him and between the two of them, they broke the door down. Once inside, Torrian's eyes immediately shot to Heather—she had crumpled to the floor, and her bodice was ripped in two.

Dugald turned to him, his eyes in a fury.

"Back, Loki," Torrian growled.

Loki moved out of the small cottage, standing in the doorway but giving Torrian the space he needed to fight his battle.

JAKE

BOOK 4

Of the second generation of Grants, Loki was closest to the twins.

CHAPTER 18

Loki and his mountains…

THEY LEFT EARLY the next morn. Kenzie rode with Loki, Aline with Jake, and Magnus rode alone. Jake kept his lips in her hair for most of the trip, taking in her scent for comfort. She smelled of lavender, most likely from the oil his aunt Celestina made.

Loki glanced up at the majestic mountain in front of them, covered in white.

"Papa, why do you stare at the mountains so?" Kenzie asked.

Loki tried to straighten the lad's unruly hair. "Must you be so attentive? I stare at the mountains because they represent freedom and a good life to me. You know exactly what I mean, do you not?"

Kenzie frowned, but then glanced around him. "Aye, but to me, 'tis something different. Why the mountains?"

"Because the first time I saw them, I rode in front of my mama, though I did not yet know that she would adopt me. We were traveling to see Da because of his injury. 'Twas verra cold and nearly winter, the snow was flying hard, and I'll never forget the first time I saw the mountains and the

Grant lists. The peaks looked like they touched the heavens. 'Twas where I thought we were headed, but the next thing I saw was the Grant lists. That *was* heaven to me. Was there not something similar for you?"

"Aye, but you will laugh at me if I tell you."

Jake listened to his cousin's conversation with his adopted son, curious to see what Kenzie would say meant the most to him. All the clan knew of Loki's attraction to the mountains, but what did the wee laddie care about?

"Go ahead." He tipped his head toward Jake. "We promise not to laugh." Magnus was too far ahead to overhear, but Jake stayed close.

"The moment I knew things might change for me was when you and Grandsire came to get me. Remember when Grandsire told me to go get my favorite animal my mama had made for me? I knew for sure you were Lucky Loki then, and I knew you would not leave me to live in a crate."

Jake turned to Kenzie. "Is there a sight that summons that feeling for you?"

"Aye, whenever I see my papa and grandsire. Then I know I'm lucky, too."

Loki gave Kenzie a quick hug and they continued onward.

LOKI'S CHRISTMAS STORY

Loki struggled to find his purpose in the world, but he needn't have worried. It found him.

CHAPTER NINE

Loki learns the origin of his name.

"BOR, MAY I speak with you outside?"

"Of course." Bor led the way out the door and, instead of stopping, walked into the nearby forest, continuing on until he came to a clearing.

He turned around, giving Loki a pointed look, but Loki had no idea what the old man wanted from him. His gaze scanned the area, a small clearing surrounded by trees on all sides. Strangely enough, something pulled to him, so he walked the perimeter without any prompting from Bor, finally stopping at a tree with multiple cut marks across it. It looked as if someone had attempted to cut it down and failed. A stump was not far from it, so he sat down, staring at the tree as visions peppered his mind.

A young lad.

An axe.

Tears.

Screams.

Howling pain—the kind of pain no healer could cure, the kind that would dig at you every day.

Every day until you wanted to quit, run away, give up.

"Do you recall anything about that tree, Lucas?"

Tears flooded his eyes as it all came back to him, flitting bits and pieces of memory tugging their way out of the recesses in his mind. "You called me Lucas. You know my true sire."

Bor stood with his hands behind his back. "I did, and I do. Tell me what you remember."

Loki stared at the tree and a young lad popped in front of him, a lad angry at the world, swinging an axe at the tree over and over and over again.

The lad screamed and screamed, "I hate you, I hate you, I hate you…"

Loki stared at Bor through his tears. "Who did I hate so badly?"

"Your father, or the man you believed to be your father, and another man."

He jumped up from the tree stump as the memories returned in full. "I was angry with my father. I hated him. He wasn't truly my father, but I didn't know it then. I tried to save my mother from a beating…"

"Instead your father and his helper beat you."

"Aye. That man, Hamish, threw me in a wagon and took me away. I recalled this before…he tossed me out of the wagon expecting me to die, but I didn't."

"Nay, you were stronger than they expected you to be. You fought hard, crawled on your hands and knees until someone found you." Bor stood unmoving, his hands still behind his back.

"You. 'Twas *you* who found me." Memories of a burly, bearded man with a smile and kind eyes flooded back to him. Bor had climbed off his horse and lifted him up, giving him water and telling him he'd not die. "You saved me, brought me to Ayr."

"I did bring you to Ayr, but you'd already saved yourself. I then brought you here to live with us. Even in this place, your desire for vengeance ate at your insides. Do you remember?"

Loki's eyes widened. "I do." He paced in a circle. "I wanted to kill Hamish. Hamish and Blackett, the rat bastard who beat my mother and pretended to be my sire. Only he wasn't. He killed my mother, I'm sure of it."

"Probably. You wished to find them and make them pay. I'd hoped you would lose some of your anger if I allowed you to swing at that tree, but it never helped, until one day…"

Loki held his hand up. "Saints above, I remember. Allow me. I swung and swung, and one day, I was so angry that I told you I didn't want to be called Lucas anymore."

"Aye, you believed it tied you to Blackett, that he'd chosen the name for you."

"I hated him, so it ate at my insides…but…" So much had returned, but it still didn't all fit together. "I wanted a new name. You told me tales of the Norse gods and goddesses, and I wanted to be just like Loki."

"Aye, you wished to be the wee trickster, and you vowed you'd become one of the largest and fiercest warriors in all the land so that you could return one day to kill Blackett and Hamish. According to your true sire, you did just that."

"I did. Blackett tricked me first, but good triumphed over evil that day. I hated those rat bastards."

"Did you defeat them alone?"

Loki settled back on the stump. "Nay, only with the help of my adoptive family, Clan Grant, and our allies, the Ramsays."

"I doubt the Grants and Ramsays come together for just anyone, do they?"

He dipped his head, thinking of how fortunate he'd been to run into Brodie Grant and Fergus's sire, Nicol. "Nay, they do not. But how did you know my true sire?"

"I met him not long ago. There are not many men who have one blue eye and one green. I asked him about you, and sure enough, he was your sire. He thanked me for picking you up from the ground where I found you."

"I remember everything, but why couldn't I recall it before? I don't understand." He rested his head in his hands, trying to work this new information into the tapestry of his life.

"Because the last day you were out here swinging, you lost your balance and hit your head on a rock. It knocked you out. When you awakened, you would only answer to Loki, and you left for Ayr the next day. That's all I can tell you. As you said to Kenzie, the mind protects itself when it must."

"I had several dreams about you recently…as did my son. Why? You are the caretaker of lost children. Why would I start dreaming about you now?"

Bor grinned. "Och, I can only thank the angels for that. I'm not sure I believe in them, but I was desperate to contact you, and I prayed for them to bring you to me."

"Why?" Loki stood up to face the old man, just now noticing how tired his eyes were, how the color of his skin had a slight yellowish cast.

Bor took a deep breath and let it out slowly, shifting his gaze from his feet back up to Loki's eyes. "Because I'll not be of this world much longer. I seek to find someone to take on my work, to keep searching for the lost souls, the weak bairns, the orphaned. Your sire told me you had your own castle, and I'd hoped you could help me."

"You want me to take all the bairns home with me now?" Loki was in shock, not sure if he could do this without first talking with his sweet Bella.

"Nay, please do not take them from me now. Bestla would be devastated. I'm not leaving yet, and you still have a challenge or two ahead of you, but I was hoping I could send a messenger to you when my time was near. And I would ask that you travel to Ayr and Edinburgh once or twice a year to find the newest lost souls, bring them to a warm home."

Loki nodded, thinking about his proposition. He knew there were many generous souls at Grant land who would gladly help him. His mother, Gracie, Kyla, Ashlyn and Magnus, Aline, and so many more. He had plenty of room in his keep, and needed to build his own people to add to the might of Clan Grant. "I'd be happy to, if you'll allow us to take Ami with us. 'Twould break Kenzie's heart to leave without her. We'll wait to leave until she's well enough to make the journey, of course."

"I can agree to that. I do not wish to lose another bairn." His sadness changed as the ends of his lips curved up ever so slightly. "So you'll come when I send a message?"

He nodded…

Chapter Ten

Loki returns home to devastating news.

They were almost home. The Grant guards surrounded them, assisting their travel through the more treacherous areas. Once they arrived at Castle Curanta, he hopped off his horse. "Forgive me," he announced to all of them, "but Jamie and Fergus will assist you from here. I must go to Bella. Jamie—" he handed Ami over to him, "—please bring her inside but 'tis verra important that you keep her warm."

With that, he raced across his courtyard and up the steps to his hall. There were few people inside, he noticed, but all were somber, including his mother. He waved at them as soon as he was inside the door and asked, "Bella?"

"Upstairs, Loki." His mother pointed to the staircase, and he chose not to focus on the sad expression on her face. Surely it just meant that Bella hadn't delivered yet, that they were overanxious waiting for the bairn to come.

He took the steps three at a time and arrived at his chamber, opening it with a knock so as not to startle his wee wife. He stepped inside, surprised to see Gracie, Aunt Caralyn, and Aunt Maddie at Bella's bedside.

He could hear her sobs under the covers, and all

he could think was the worst. Their bairn. What had happened to their bairn?

"Aunt Maddie?" he whispered.

She strode over to his side and took his hands in hers. Caralyn grasped his shoulders. "Loki," she said, "Bella lost the bairn. I'm so sorry."

Gracie came over and gave him a quick hug, mumbling some kind words, but he didn't hear them. His gaze was focused on Bella's shape under the covers.

He heard the door close behind him as the women left, so he moved over and sat on the edge of the bed. "Bella?"

She finally popped out and threw her arms around him. "Loki, I'm so sorry, so sorry. Forgive me."

He hugged her to him, wrapping his arms around her tightly and taking in her sweet scent, which reminded him that he was home. They had lost the babe, but she was safe. "What happened? Why are you apologizing?"

She pulled back, her breath hitching between sobs. "I lost the babe. 'Twas a wee lassie, and she never took a breath."

"But why are you apologizing? 'Tis not your fault."

"Because I should have told you, but I couldn't. I just couldn't. I didn't want to believe it."

"Believe what?"

"The bairn had stopped moving in my belly." She wailed two more times before she could stop crying long enough to talk again. "I loved her so much, and I didn't wish to admit she was gone. But Caralyn had told me a sennight before you left to pay attention to the babe's movement. The babe stopped moving before you left…and she was born two days afterward. She never took a breath. I held her close and we had to bury her while you were gone. I'm so sorry. I should have told you."

"Och, sweet Belle. Do not apologize. *I'm* sorry. I wish I had been here with you. You should not have gone through it all alone."

"Oh, Loki, she was so beautiful. I wished for a way to breathe life into her, but there was no hope. She was so tiny."

Loki held Bella while she sobbed, not knowing what else to do. They'd lost a daughter. After all he'd just been through, he couldn't help but ask why this would happen now.

"Husband, Caralyn said there is a way to keep me from carrying again. She has herbs to give me. I don't know if I can go through this again. 'Twas so painful. I hope you're not upset with me. I tried to be a good mama and eat well so she would be a big bairn, but I failed. She says we can change our minds later, but I could not handle carrying again right away. Please?"

He cupped her face. "Hush, never say such things." He kissed her tenderly, hoping to let her know how much he loved her. "Bella, you are a wonderful mother to Lucas. We have a wonderful, strong laddie, we have Kenzie, and if you wish to take the herbs, then do it. 'Twas no fault of yours. I don't believe such drivel. 'Tis God's way…and mayhap 'tis not for us to question."

A strange feeling washed over him. He didn't believe God had purposefully taken this babe from them, but mayhap He had known it would happen… mayhap that was why He'd sent the dreams to him and Kenzie. What if they hadn't gone? They would never have met Bor, never have arranged to take his place as the helpers of lost children, never have met wee Ami…

Fear gripped him as he thought about Ami downstairs. How would Bella react to the wee lass after losing her own bairn? The possibility of this loss had never occurred to him when he'd agreed to bring Ami home. Before he had time to give it any more thought, Kenzie's face peeked around the corner of the door.

"Papa, may I bring her in to meet Mama?"

Loki stared at Bella, not knowing how to tell her what they'd done. Ultimately, though, he had no choice but to speak. "Bella, the lass lost her mama. She doesn't speak, and she had no one but an old woman and old man to care for her. Had I known you'd lost the babe, I would not have brought her to you, but she fell in love with Kenzie, and he wanted to bring her home, make her part of our family. If you don't want…"

Bella stared at him in astonishment, but then brought her finger up to his lips to quiet him. She waved to Kenzie. "You brought a bairn home with you?"

"Aye, Mama," Kenzie said. "Aunt Maddie told me about the bairn, and I'm so sorry, but Ami had no one, and she loves me, so I thought she could come home with us and be my sister. She needs a mama, and since you are the best mama in the world…" He pulled Ami in through the door. She stood next to Kenzie, gripping his leg, her thumb in her mouth as she sucked away.

Loki looked at Bella, not knowing what else to say. Her hand fell away from Loki's lips, and she waved for Kenzie to bring the lass closer. "How old is she?" Bella asked.

Kenzie stood next to the bed, Ami still gripping his arm. "Her name is Ami and she's only two summers. She's verra sweet, Mama."

Ami let go of Kenzie's leg and stood up straight, yanking her thumb out of her mouth. She looked straight at Bella and held her arms up to her.

She finally spoke her first word.

"Mama?"

ELIZABETH

BOOK 12

Elizabeth falls in love with Gil, the lad who helped Finlay save Kyla. Gil lives at Castle Curanta with Loki.

CHAPTER 9

Loki and his band of orphans find a few more.

GIL STAYED A distance behind Loki, in the hopes he wouldn't keep commenting on the lavender aroma wafting from his purchase. Though he did his best to focus his thoughts on Lizzie, he failed. His mind couldn't stop returning to the man he'd seen back at the vendor stalls. Could it have been Morgan?

He hadn't gotten a really good look at the man, so he'd convinced himself he was wrong. He'd jumped to conclusions because his fears and emotions were driving him, something a warrior should never allow to happen.

He blamed the entire event on his imagination.

Either way, the possible sighting had distracted him more than he wished to admit. So when two lads boldly pushed through Loki, Thorn, and Nari, they were taken totally off-guard. Gil was the only one who noticed that one of them snagged a bag of coins from Loki's pocket.

"Loki, your coin!" Gil shouted, racing after the lad of around seven winters.

Loki must have finally noticed because he was suddenly directly behind the lad. The two lads had run off in different directions, but Gil and Loki stayed with the wee thief. Nari and Thorn took off after the other.

He led them down a deserted pathway surrounded by trees. It was Loki who caught him, grabbing his collar and lifting him off the ground into the air. It wasn't long before Thorn and Nari found the other one and dragged him over, cursing and kicking.

Loki placed his hand on the hilt of his sword and said, "Both of you on the boulder and do not move."

The moment they saw his weapon, they backed up with no further complaints. "Return my coin, you wee thieves," he insisted.

"I dinnae know him," the first one said, glaring at the younger one as he crossed his arms.

"The hell you don't. He is your partner in crime. Return my coin." Loki leaned forward, using one of his favorite intimidation tactics.

The lad shook his head vehemently. "I have no coin. I know no' what ye're talking 'bout."

Loki motioned to Gil, and the two picked the lad up, Loki grabbing his hands while Gil took his feet, and shook him. Nothing happened. Loki made another motion to Gil, who hoisted his feet higher, turning him upside down until the coin bag fell from his trews.

"You wee thief. I know 'tis my bag because it has my initials sewn in it." Loki picked it up and made sure the coins were all inside before indicating to Gil that he could set the lad down.

"Why are you stealing?" Loki asked. "Where are your parents?"

"We don't have parents." By the look of their

grimy faces and dirty clothing, Gil had to believe he was telling the truth. "Who needs them anyway?" He cast a disgusted look at Loki.

"Tell me the truth about why you're stealing. I'll feed you if you're hungry, but even growing lads like you don't need this much coin to eat."

Loki planted his feet apart and stood in front of the one who'd taken his coin, his arms crossed. The lad joined his friend back on the rock.

The smallest of the two, a lad with red hair and freckles, started to cry. The older one said, "Shush, you wee bairn."

The lad bawled on, sputtering out a few words they could make out here and there. "Kill…catch us…dinnae want….to die."

"Lad," Thorn said, moving closer. "We'll not kill you. We were all orphans, too."

The older one looked flummoxed by the news, but the small one kept wailing. "They said if we make enough coin for them, they'll take us to a nice place for orphans."

Gil was surprised to hear that word of Loki's work had traveled all the way into Edinburgh, though they did journey there at least once a year. It infuriated him to think they'd been used as incentive for thievery, especially since he had little doubt the men behind this had no intention of following through.

"Stop," he said to the laddie. "We'll not kill you." Hearing him carry on so tore a hole in his heart. Though he'd been older when his family had passed on, closer to the older one's age, he'd felt like the wee lad in front of him.

Alone with no one to help him, no one to feed him, no one to talk with. He wasn't surprised to see the wee one with the older one. What would have happened to him otherwise? "How do you know each other?"

"I protect him," the larger boy said. "He's too small to be alone. And there are really mean people out there."

But the wee one kept sobbing.

Finally, the older one said, "He's not afraid of you killing us."

"But I am afraid," the small one said, sniffling. "I'm afraid to die, even if you're not. I'm afraid of all of them."

"Out with it," Loki said firmly. "Who are you working for and who do you fear will kill you?"

The thief finally said, "Will you buy us each a meat pie if we tell?"

Loki nodded.

"We work for a man who lives in a castle beyond the walls, from far away. He leaves men in Edinburgh who watch over us and make us steal. They feed us, but hardly enough. My belly is always growling."

Gil recognized what the lad wasn't saying. "You give the laddie some of your food, do you not?" He would have done the same.

The lad continued, "We never see the man in charge, but he tells the others whether or not to beat us. Some of them beat us whenever they wish, though. They don't care if we deserve it or not."

Simon had been like that. He'd never understood what set him off—if he'd known, he would have stopped the behavior. Eventually, he'd decided the bastard swung out whenever he was angry, and he didn't care who he hurt.

"So we steal," the lad said. "My apologies to you."

Loki looked from Gil to Thorn and Nari. "Sounds familiar. I recall men trying to make me steal, but I always got away from them."

"We'll take you with us," Gil blurted out, remembering a time when he'd wandered these streets, alone and desperate. Remembering where he'd ended up before finding the Grants. He didn't want that for these lads. "We live in a castle for orphans. 'Tis as we said. We're all orphans."

The wee one stopped crying and whispered, "Ye will? Who runs the castle?"

"They're telling you lies," the thief said. "I've asked the nuns, and they said the only place they know that takes in all orphans is Castle Curanta, way up in the Highlands. She thought there was another one, too, but it's even farther in the Highlands."

"Mayhap they are not lying, Daw," the wee one insisted.

"Shut your mouth, Herry," he replied.

Loki smirked and asked, "What else do you know of that castle?"

"'Tis run by Loki, the orphan adopted by the Grant warriors," Daw said with wonder. "He was such a good fighter in the Battle of Largs that the Grants gave him his verra own castle. He was adopted, and now he's a Grant."

Daw, who had dark hair, turned to Herry, whose red hair looked nearly brown from the dirt. "'Tis where we wish to go, but we don't know how to get there. The one man said he'd take us there once we steal enough for them."

Loki had a smug grin on his face, and he gave Gil a slight nod. Tempted to grin himself, Gil said, "Did you look at the initials inside the bag you took?"

"I cannot read letters," Daw barked.

"I can," Herry volunteered. "My Mama taught me my letters afore she passed from the fever. I was just beginning to read. May I look at the letters, my lord?" Herry asked.

Loki held the bag out for the lad, holding the initials up to his face. His eyes widened, and he slowly lifted his gaze to Loki.

"Aye, Daw. It says what you think it does."

"What are the letters?" Daw asked.

Herry whispered, "L for Loki and G for Grant."

"You read them correctly, lad. My dear lady sewed them carefully inside all my bags. My name is Loki, and I lived in a crate behind a tavern in Ayr before the Grants came along and took me with them."

"You were truly adopted by the great Alexander Grant?" Daw asked, his ill temper washing away as awe filled his eyes.

"Nay, I was adopted by his brother, Brodie, and his wife, Celestina. They are my adoptive parents." He sat down on a nearby boulder and rested an elbow on his knee. "But 'twas Alexander Grant who gave me Castle Curanta."

"And every year we come to Edinburgh for orphans," Nari added. "We'll take you with us if you wish. You can live in our castle."

Herry ran over and hugged Nari. "I want to go. I hate those men."

Then he glanced back at Daw for his reaction. He didn't answer quickly, instead slowly taking the measure of each of them. After a long pause, Daw said, "We'll both go, but only if you train us to be Grant warriors."

"Deal," Loki said. "Anything else you need?"

Gil did his best not to laugh at Loki. He knew how to handle young lads. He sat down on a log, memories washing through him. After he'd gotten Kyla back to Cameron land, Chief Cameron had taken him right into the kitchens and told him he could eat whatever he wanted. Gil thought he'd landed in heaven. Cameron keep had impressed him, but not as much as Castle Curanta.

The first time he sat at the trestle table with the other lads and lassies, they shared how they'd lost their parents. Loki came along and told them his story, something that made him realize he was finally where he belonged.

He'd made fast friends who'd never deserted him, Kenzie being his first. Kenzie had taken Gil along everywhere for the first fortnight, showing him everything. To this day, he was still Gil's closest friend.

"Grant plaids," Daw shouted excitedly. "Can we wear Grant plaids?"

"I'll have our seamstress fit them to you. And new trews for winter, along with a tunic or two."

The first time Gil had donned a Grant plaid and gone out to the lists to train, he'd finally felt as if he belonged.

Herry swiped the tears from his face, leaving a dirty streak across one cheek. He held his foot up and asked, "May I have new boots when we get to the Highlands, my lord?"

Gil was caught by the sight of the lad's toes pushing out of the seam of the boot toe. "Nay," he said, before Loki could answer. The lad was about to start crying again when Gil knelt down in front of him. Up close, he'd guess him to be no more than five winters. "Nay, Herry. We'll get you the boots now. I'll take both of you. You'll need good ones to get to the Highlands. And new woolen hose, too."

Eyes shining with tears and happiness, Herry jumped up and hugged him.

Thorn added, "And we'll protect you from the cruel bastards who forced you to steal."

"I promise no one at Castle Curanta will beat you," Loki said. "Ever. What say you? Say aye, and we'll head to the meat pie vendor."

Herry nodded quickly, while Daw took several seconds to agree. But he did it with a smile.

Once they filled their bellies, Loki strode down to an inn, entered, and said, "We'll be staying the night. One large room with four pallets and two for the wee ones." Thorn had held back to speak with the guards, making plans for the warriors to sleep in the town stables.

The innkeeper stepped away for a moment, and Herry pulled on Loki's shirt and whispered, "We don't have to sleep in the stables this eve, my lord?"

Loki patted the top of his head and said, "Nay, lad. From here on, we'll keep you warm each night. Sometimes we huddle in a cave together, but you'll be you warm."

Gil swore he saw tears misting the bairn's eyes.

While the other had toughened, this lad clearly had not.

As if Loki could read his mind, he whispered over his shoulder. "Poor lad stayed with them for protection and to stay alive is my guess."

Gil held his hand out, and it surprised him how quickly Herry grabbed it. He led him over to the hearth, the crackling flames inviting in the chilly front chamber only meant for welcoming guests.

Once the innkeeper returned and the arrangements were finalized, Loki nodded to the man. "We'll return, but we're heading to the bathhouse first." Then he turned to glance at the lads, one at a time. "You smell. Both of you. Grant warriors don't smell."

Gil was distracted right away, memories of Sabina fresh in his mind. A vendor with fabric animals was straight ahead so he knew what he had to do. He reached the stall and picked up a gray dog who looked like a deerhound, paid for it, and handed it over to Herry, whose face lit up. "For me? May I keep it?"

"Aye, 'tis yours, lad. Daw, you need one, too?"

Daw, looking quite offended, said, "Nay, I'm too old."

HIGHLAND RETRIBUTION

BOOK 3

BRADEN AND CAIRSTINE
Loki helps protect the bairns from the Channel of Dubh.

CHAPTER SEVENTEEN

The men from the channel bring a group of bairns to be shipped across the water. But The Band of Cousins are there to stop it. Loki's sling does it again, this time in the Channel of Dubh.

Kenzie has faith that Loki, his adoptive sire, will save him and the others.

IT HAD BEEN terribly difficult for Steenie to mind his tongue with the men who'd come to put them in a cart and carry them through the mountains toward the loch. The one trail had been so treacherous that the wee bairns had cried for their mamas over and over again, and the four men traveling with them had not been kind. They'd cussed at them so much that Steenie had wished to hit each of them with his fist. He wanted his arms to be like tree trunks like Robbie and Braden Grant's so he could punch them and make them stop being so mean.

He flexed his muscles to check them out, wondering how he could get them to be so big.

"You have to work in the Grant lists, Steenie," Kenzie whispered.

"Huh?"

"I saw you looking at your muscles. You want them big like the Grants, do you not?"

Steenie nodded, his face lighting up. "Aye, how can I get them that big?"

"You have to work in the lists. They work there every day."

"Can I when we get out? I'll get mine to be bigger." He flexed his one arm to demonstrate to Kenzie how big his was already.

Kenzie said with a grin, "When you're a wee bit older, mayhap."

"I'll practice every day." He was sure he could get his arms to be bigger.

Before he knew it, they'd made it through and were drawing near the loch.

When they could see the loch ahead, Kenzie leaned over to whisper to Steenie. "If you see any hawks or falcons overhead, especially more than one, 'tis a good sign."

"Why?" Steenie whispered.

"Because my cousin married the Wild Falconer and Uncle Alex sent for them, though 'tis unlikely they're here yet. But Papa says they do amazing things. Have you not heard about him?"

Steenie shook his head, his eyes widening. "What does he do?"

"He can send his birds down to attack mean people. They've done it before and 'tis spectacular. If you see them, it means my cousins are here."

"You two lads keep quiet back there. I shoulda split you two up." The lead man had a long scruffy beard that hit his chest.

"Scruffy..." Steenie whispered. Then he looked at

Kenzie and giggled. That was one of the activities that had helped them make it through the night—giving names to all of their captors. Scruffy, Blackteeth, Stubby—because he'd lost two fingers—and Smelly.

He peeked at the two lassies in the cart with them. They were sisters, and one had her head in her sister's lap while she sucked her thumb. "Why does she suck her thumb still? I don't."

"Because she watched her mother die not long ago. She's sucked it ever since," the girl named Edith said bluntly. She turned her head away from Steenie, and he wondered if she was mad he'd asked such a direct question.

"What's her name?" he asked, hoping to get her to talk to him again. He would feel horrible if he lost his mother, especially if something happened to her in front of him and he wasn't able to stop it.

"Eva."

"How old is she?"

"She's eight summers."

"How did you get here?"

"Two of these men came and killed our mother, then stole us from my aunt. We were living with her." She wiped the tears that formed in the corners of her eyes. "Do you know where they're taking us?"

"Nay, but do not worry," Kenzie said. "My sire will save us. Watch for the falcons and slingers."

"Slingers?" she whispered.

"Aye. My sire is the best. He slings small rocks at bad men."

A bold voice shouted back at them from the front. "I said keep quiet. All of you."

Kenzie held his finger up to his lips. Steenie

scowled, but there was naught they could do but listen. Both lads tipped their heads back, and Steenie hoped he'd see a bunch of wild falcons.

He wished to meet the Wild Falconer. Maybe someday he could *be* a Wild Falconer.

There weren't any falcons in eyesight, so Steenie shifted his gaze to the path ahead of them, just then realizing he could see the loch. He pointed his finger toward the water, and Kenzie glanced over his shoulder to follow. When they came down the hill, there was a large clearing on one side of the loch with a couple of small huts near one end. He could see clear across to the other side because it was so big.

He didn't like the boat at the edge. Two men were stacking crates around the lip of the loch while three men worked on the boat, getting water, sweeping the boat out, spitting over the edge.

He watched the man spit over and over again. Someday he'd be able to spit that far. He decided to practice a bit, so he spat over the side of the cart to see how far it would go. He did this for a while until Kenzie poked him in his back.

He peered over his shoulder at Kenzie, who pointed up to the sky. He was careful to make sure no one else saw what he was doing, so Steenie guessed it was important. He tipped his head up toward the gray sky, but he didn't see anything at first. A moment later, two big birds soared above them, sweeping lower and lower.

He couldn't help but clap his hands.

"What the hell is with the birds? They've been following us for the last quarter hour," Stubby yelled.

Scruffy shouted back at him. "Who cares? They're just birds, you daft arse." Then he spat to the side of his horse.

Steenie giggled and whispered, "Daft arse." Then he spat over the side, pleased that it was farther than his previous marks.

Blackteeth pulled the first cart full of girls, also carrying Hilda, into the clearing, waving to the men aboard the boat. Then he cursed and slapped the back of his head. Spinning around on his horse, he stared at Scruffy who was mounted behind him.

"What the hell? Why are you throwing stones at me?"

Kenzie pulled on Steenie's tunic, wide-eyed. He whispered, "My sire. He's here!"

Scruffy said, "I didn't throw naught at you, but I will if you don't keep moving."

The two men who'd ridden by themselves climbed down and moved over to the cart in front, lifting the lassies out one by one and pushing them toward the boat. One of the men roared as his head was jerked backward. "Who did that?" he shouted, his hand flying up to his forehead.

Steenie watched as Kenzie pulled out his own slinger, stuck a rock in it and sent it flying at the man who'd been in the first cart, hitting him in the back of the head. "I grabbed the stones when we got into the cart when the men weren't looking," he explained with a whisper.

Blackteeth turned on Scruffy and shouted, "You bastard. 'Tis the second time you've hit me. Come over here and try it. I'll kick your arse."

Scruffy got hit in the back of his head next. "I

didn't do naught," he said, "but somebody just hit me."

The other cart had emptied, but Kenzie, Steenie, Edith, and Eva were still in their cart when the falcons dipped down from the sky again, soaring over the entire group of them.

"Kenzie, look. 'Tis the falcons again just like you said," Steenie whispered.

Their captors, nine in all—the four who'd brought them here and the five near the boat—started jabbering and shouting. Hilda must have sensed an opportunity, for she sent the girls running toward the huts at the end, but they were so confused, they ran in different directions.

All of a sudden, three horses carrying men with red plaids charged out of the woods. Kenzie grabbed Eva out of Edith's arms and said, "Run!"

Steenie hopped out of the cart and ran for the trees as fast as his wee legs could carry him. He knew those plaids.

The Grants had come.

Chapter Eighteen

Maggie had led Braden and the others down a rarely used path to the loch. He (Braden) couldn't help but smile when he noticed Loki ahead of him, his slinger in hand. The others were gathered behind him. His brother was sheer magic with his slinger, able to catapult small rocks long distances with dead aim. He'd been doing it since he was young and living alone behind an inn.

Cairstine started to speak, but he squeezed her

hip and covered her mouth. He pointed down to the loch, where he could just barely see the boat through the trees. It looked like there were several bairns in the clearing.

He heard Cairstine gasp.

"We found him. 'Tis what's important," he reminded her with a whisper. "And now we'll get him to safety." She spun around and nodded, her lips sealed.

They all took their places, not needing to converse with each other because they had planned their roles in advance. Gavin, Will, and Gregor would find perches where they could back the ground crew up with arrows, while Loki, Connor, and Roddy would use their swords, and Braden and Maggie would go scoop up the bairns, the archers protecting them. Usually Braden preferred sword-to-sword combat, but he was grateful Maggie had suggested this change. His body could only endure so much.

"What about Loki's group?" Braden had asked before they set out.

Maggie had snorted, quite like a man, and said, "Loki planned to leave his guards at the top of the hill to search for any other men in the area before he joined us. He and Connor and Roddy are probably the best swordsmen in the Highlands. They don't need any instructions. With our three swordsmen and three archers, we can easily take on nine men."

Cairstine gave him a questioning look and said, "Nine to six?"

Braden grinned. "You've not seen all the Grants fight before, so I'll ignore that question. Do not worry about it. I'll bring the bairns to you, all of them. Can you handle it?"

She nodded. "Aye, absolutely."

Loki had worked his magic on the men near the boats, who had begun to argue and grab the backs of their heads. Braden moved close to Maggie and helped Cairstine dismount. "I'm leaving you behind in this small group of trees," he said to her, stroking her back. "You'll be safe. Maggie and I will stay on our horses, the others will fight on foot. When we grab the bairns, we'll bring them back to you. Just keep them hidden and safe until this is over."

She nodded, wringing her hands as she watched the activity by the loch. He understood how difficult it was for her to stay put and not go chasing after Steenie.

His cousins let their famous Grant war whoop loose, and chaos descended as they dismounted and went after the four bastards who'd smuggled the children. All of them were now on foot. He glanced at Cairstine one more time, the trust and hope in her gaze humbling him, then flicked the reins of his horse and flew into the middle of the clearing. The first thing he noticed was a wee lassie running in circles, so he headed straight for her, but she was too low to the ground for him to reach her. Then he saw Kenzie running toward him with a lass in his arms. "Here," he yelled. "Hand the lassie up to me."

Kenzie helped both lassies get settled on the horse.

"This way," Braden said to him. "Run on this side of my horse so the archers won't catch you." He turned his horse back toward the trees while Kenzie raced along next to him. Once he was out of range, he handed the two lassies to Cairstine and spoke to Kenzie. "Help her, lad. Maggie is bringing more." Then he turned back and headed toward the loch again once he noticed an older woman running with more bairns around her.

He saw Steenie at the same time Cairstine's scream carried to him. A man was running behind the lad, his sword arched over his head.

"Circle, Braden!" Gavin's instructions gave him exactly the information he needed, telling him how to approach and leave a shot for the archer.

He headed toward Steenie, who'd finally noticed him, and yelled, "Arms up, Steenie." Fortunately, the wee laddie understood him. He stuck both hands into the air and Braden leaned over and grabbed him by the waist. He feared he was going to lose him, but he said, "Grab my neck, Steenie." Then he circled around the attacker while Steenie grappled for balance on the horse. A second later an arrow sluiced through the air and caught the fool now in front of them square in the neck.

Steenie clutched him so tightly he had to say, "Let go, lad. I need to breathe." The look of relief on the lad's face released a knot of tension in his chest. The wee laddie was away from the kidnappers, and he'd soon be safe with his mama. Aside from Steenie loosening his grip, Braden could breathe again knowing that he'd fulfilled his promises to Cairstine. He'd show her he was a man of his word time and time again, starting with his latest vow to get to know her better once this war was over.

Braden headed to the trees and dropped Steenie into Cairstine's waiting arms.

"Mama! You're safe," Steenie said as she grabbed him and hugged him tight.

Braden's chest puffed out as he watched the two together. Cairstine glanced his way, such gratitude in her eyes that he was humbled.

But he couldn't wait any longer, so he swung back around. They really had no idea how many bairns were there. The number of enemies still swinging their swords was down from nine to five, though two had decided to give up and fled back to their boat.

Braden saw Maggie grab one of the small lassies, but he noticed one of the older ones was spinning around in a panic of confusion, gripping a young girl in her arms. It was obvious she didn't know where to run or who to trust. He shouted, "Hand her to me." The girl, crying furiously, held the wee lass up so Braden could grab her. Then he slowed, "Give me your hand and you can climb on behind me."

The lass stopped crying and let out a piercing scream unlike anything he'd ever heard before. Braden had no idea how to calm her. Then Cairstine's voice carried across the distance to him and the girl. "Edith, trust him."

Hell, but Cairstine knew the lass?

Edith must have recognized Cairstine, too, because she offered her hand to Braden and he tugged her up high enough that she could slide her leg over the horse behind him. Once she was steady, he led his horse away from the few battling men and over to the trees.

Once he set her feet on the ground, Edith, still in a panic, screamed, "Eva, where are you?"

Cairstine stepped out and said, "Here, Edith. She must be here." She pointed to the three lassies behind her, all of them now sobbing.

Edith shot over to the group, picking up her sister and holding her tight, sobbing uncontrollably. Then she turned to Cairstine and looked at her, but there was no recognition in her eyes.

"Edith," she said, "I'm Cairstine...your cousin."

THE SCOT'S QUEST

BOOK 4

DYNA AND DERRIC

Loki is called to assist an old friend and mentor.

CHAPTER SIXTEEN

Alex makes a decision to save his family. His plan needs the trickster.

ALEXANDER GRANT STOOD in the middle of the forest, talking to the person whose assistance he'd sought.

"Are you sure about this?" the other asked.

"Aye. I aim to put an end to this. They stole my grandson, my daughter, and they've put my family through hell trying to get to me. DeFry and Busby came to MacLintock land and said Edward's son will not stop until he has my head."

"You think giving him what he wants is the answer?"

"I've lived a full life. I'll not have a young life lost over my old one. This must end now. I had to choose carefully, but I've known you for many years. I believe you will assist me in this endeavor. I only have one caveat."

"And what is that?"

"You must tell no one. Will you agree?"

The man who stood in front of him thought carefully, something he should do. He knew what this action would bring down upon him. All the

Grants would come for him if they learned the truth.

But Alex trusted this man, trusted him with his life. He would do the right thing.

The man turned to him and clasped his shoulder.

"Aye, I'll assist you. Whatever it takes. I owe you much."

Alex Grant smiled and let out the breath he'd been holding.

This would end now.

Chapter Seventeen

Alex meets with the man he asked to assist him in turning himself in to the King of England. Who is the secret man? Loki, maybe?

Alex Grant rode to his destination with the man he'd chosen to assist him. They were about two hours away when the skies opened up. A thick grove of pines was nearby, and they raced under the trees as fast as they could. His partner pointed to a large overhang where they could hide from the storm, an outcropping large enough for three men and their mounts.

The sky turned black, thunder clouds rolling in every direction.

The other man asked, "Have you ever seen clouds like that before? They're going in opposite directions, something I've not witnessed."

Alex got his horse under the stone protection and dismounted, patting Midnight down to console him. Although he was stalwart and footsure in battle, the beast had always reacted badly to thunderstorms, the quaking of the ground too much for him. He whispered sweet words to the animal and pulled out an apple from his saddlebag. The horse took it quickly and munched away, the treat calming him for a wee bit.

Alex set his hands on his hips, staring up at the thunderstorm raging around them. "I have seen one storm like this, and it was not from anything good. It meant evil was trying to steal a sapphire sword belonging to the fae."

"When did it happen?" the other man asked.

"Avelina Ramsay had control of the sword. She fought with a daft man over it. Her brother told me the storm started because she held the sword overhead. She was driving a man with ill intent away from her. I've never seen another sight like it. Howbeit…" He couldn't help but think of his granddaughter, Dyna. Blessed with the talents of a seer and the odd ability to pull power into her cousins' swords by holding her bow over her head, he began to see a similarity between her talents and those of Avelina Ramsay. Was there more to the spectral swords than he realized? And what part was Dyna playing in this unnatural storm?

He wondered where she was and who was with her. Then another thought thrust itself into his mind. The sapphire sword. His sister Brenna had said something about a challenge arising every fifty years. Their mother had told Brenna and Jennie about it, about how a fae queen would choose a mortal being when necessary to help save the Scots, but only when all else had failed.

He pushed his memory back to it, trying to remember all he'd learned, how Brenna had told him that Gregor had been near death, but that Avelina had held him and breathed life back into him.

The fae had given her special powers along with the sword. Avelina had fought against evil and won, and the fae queen had told her to hide the sword, that she would return when it was needed again. That was it. The fae queen had said there would be peace for a time, but eventually they would need to fight evil in Scotland again.

Was the time nigh?

"I wonder. Has it been fifty years?" He said it loud enough to be heard, though he hadn't meant to because anyone who heard him was bound to think him daft.

Then he shook his head, chastising himself for seeing things that weren't there. Besides, it couldn't have been more than forty years.

"What is it?" his companion asked.

"Naught," Alex replied. "Musings of an old man, one who wishes to believe his wife comes to him in his dreams and his grandchildren have special talents."

"Like an orphan dreams of being adopted someday?"

Alex glanced at him and grinned. "Something like that."

The two men watched the wild gusting of the wind, the sheeting rain drenching the landscape, the thunder coming so quickly it was impossible to anticipate the claps.

Alex whispered to himself, "Never seen another like it until now."

The other man stared at him.

"And I don't like it."

Chapter Twenty

Alex plans to give himself to King Edward in return for the promise to leave his family alone. He cannot do it without his confidante.

Alexander Grant was tired. Tired of searching over half the Highlands for the person he sought. It wouldn't be long before someone from his clan found him and he'd be forced to go back to Grant land.

But he couldn't.

He was done watching his clan be tortured by the English.

The last plan he'd made had failed—the Scottish sheriffs hadn't been stationed near King Robert like he'd thought. His confidant had done as promised, but he couldn't keep asking for help.

It was time to complete this mission.

He awakened early that morn and stood on his favorite vantage point, looking down at the snow-topped Highland mountains he so loved. He only knew one person who liked this view more than he did.

His companion joined him. "'Tis a view I've always loved, but you know that. We've seen much happen in the Highlands over the years, and I still treasure every single trip I've made across this point."

Alex clasped the man's shoulder. "Aye, we've seen

much. I'd hoped to see Scotland back in control of the Scots before I leave this land. I hope King Robert will be successful. This move I'm about to make should seal that for all of our countrymen."

The other man pointed. "Look below. The ones you're searching for are there, I believe."

Alex squinted, cursing his loss of vision. "I cannot see that far any longer. I must depend on your eyes."

"Trust me that the man you are looking for is ahead of us. 'Tis time for us to move."

Alexander Grant smiled and squared his shoulders. "Lead on. We'll end this."

Chapter Twenty-Two

Loki finds Dyna, explaining his plan with Alex. How many readers guessed Alex's co-conspirator's identity?

Loki Grant grinned, leading her back off the main path and shouting over his shoulder, "Kenzie, get her horse." He rode to a hidden clearing that had been concealed behind a thick line of trees. A quick glance told her Derric was following directly behind them. "I'm sorry for surprising you, but you would have ruined our plan."

"What are you doing here?" she asked, jumping down from his horse as he soon as they slowed down. "We have to go after Grandsire." When he finally dismounted and stood in front of her, she shoved at him.

Loki just gave her a sly grin. "Uncle Alex came to me after he left Cameron land. He wanted to make sure the English wouldn't kidnap any more Grants just to get to him." He stood there with his hands on his hips, over two score of warriors behind him, all wearing Grant plaids.

They had help.

"He told you? Why did he not tell me?" Her insides twisted and turned at the thought that her grandfather trusted Loki more than her.

Apparently, she did a poor job hiding her feelings because Loki took one look at her and said, "Mayhap he asked me because he wanted to come at the English with a different force. They'd know to watch the Clan Grant warriors on your land, but no one would suspect my involvement. The English are quite ignorant, as you know. The man had his reasons," Loki said, patting her shoulder. "He asked for my assistance, and after all he's done for me, I certainly couldn't turn him down." As a bairn, Loki had been adopted by Alex's brother, Brodie, and his wife, Celestina, after they found him living in a crate behind a tavern. Alex Grant had given him his own castle, Castle Curanta, where he and his wife, Bella, took in other orphans and abandoned children. They also had two bairns of their own, a lad and a lassie.

"What exactly did he ask you to do?" Derric asked, jumping down from his horse. Then, as if realizing he had yet to introduce himself, he nodded. "Derric Corbett, pleased to meet you. I'm relieved we'll have your assistance in getting Alex Grant away from the English."

"Aye, we'll take care of them soon enough. Alex asked me not to tell anyone from his clan what he was planning until it was too late to stop him. I know you're upset he didn't confide in you, but if he had told you, you would have needed to tell your sire, your laird, his siblings, his children, and so on. I didn't have to tell anyone, so I could do what he asked without upsetting his clan and all his allies. Don't take it too hard, Dyna. But I think I'm safe revealing the truth now." He glanced back over his shoulder. "Uncle Alex told me to take the garrison out and leave no survivors. He aims to send a message, and that's exactly what we'll do."

Dyna turned to the sea of warriors that had been gathering behind Loki. She recognized many of them, and the sight brought tears to her eyes. She didn't swipe her tears away this time, instead allowing them to roll freely down her cheeks. She smiled and said, "Derric, on the left is Kenzie, next to him is Gillie, then you'll see Thorn and Nari, who helped my mother and father escape some cruel bastards. And he"—she pointed to one of the four—"is married to my aunt Elizabeth."

"You're going to attack soon?" Derric asked.

"Aye, we will. Dyna, why are you the only Grant here? I hardly think your grandsire would approve. He was expecting to see the rest of your group."

"Alasdair and Emmalin, Els and Joya, and Alick and Branwen will be along soon. They've been trailing us down the mountain. They'll help for certes."

"Any archers besides you?"

"Aye, Branwen and Emmalin." Emmalin had worked hard to build her skills, Dyna helping to train her whenever she visited MacLintock land. Joya was best at distraction.

Loki let out a low whistle. "Alex has told me about the spectral swords. I hope we get to witness you at full strength. But wee John and Ailith are safe?"

"Aye, they are on MacLintock land. Tell us what to do."

Loki stepped out of the trees to glance down the path. "We'll follow shortly, but you archers can go ahead if you can find your place quietly. We'll take them out from behind so they'll know not what hit them. Alex said he'll make his way to the front so as not to be close to the fighting. He suspected he'd be bound at this point."

"Loki, I'm so glad to see you. We'll get him back for sure."

"Aye, we will. We'll start without your cousins and hope they join us."

"How many in the garrison?" Derric asked.

Loki spit on the ground in front of him. "This is a small group. There are around four score surly Englishmen by my count to our five and forty, but we can take them. Especially if your cousins join us."

"Lead on," Dyna said, mounting her horse.

Her intuition had brought her straight to Loki. The situation was finally tilting in their favor.

THE SCOT'S DESTINY

BOOK 5

MAITLAND AND MAEVE

CHAPTER SIX

Loki stops for a night at Menzie land and meets Wiley and Q.

MAITLAND STAYED ANOTHER day before heading back to Grant land. He could simply stay through Yule—he'd planned to come here for the festive season anyway—but he had unfinished business back at Grant Castle. He wanted to take Maeve a Yuletide gift, and he knew in his heart his mother was right. He and Maeve belonged together. They could work with Maeve's disinclination to leave Grant land.

And now that he'd acknowledged his feelings for her, he did not want to delay. Neither of them were young. Which meant they didn't have much time to waste second-guessing or playing coy. And they knew what to expect out of life.

Not much.

Maitland sat on a large boulder at the Menzie archery field, an old shield fashioned into a target on a post a short distance away. He'd been working with the lads on learning to use their slings. Q was perhaps a wee bit young yet—he'd managed to hit himself with his stones as often as the target. But they all knew the story of Loki and how he'd been adopted by Brodie Grant after they found him and that he'd fought in the Battle of Largs using his sling and knocked out a few Norsemen.

Wiley let fly a stone three times and hit the target once. "Why am I missing?"

Q said, "Do dat way, Wi." He'd shortened his brother's name, just as Wiley had shortened his when he hadn't been able to say *Quillan*.

"Do what?" Maitland asked Q.

Wiley shook his head. "Not *do*. HHe said *go*. 'Go that way.' He wants me to try from this side."

Maitland glanced over at Q, who was grinning and nodding. The two had the same blond hair that carried a wee bit of wave when the wind messed it up. And they understood each other better than anyone. Like most brothers, Maitland reckoned.

"I'll try it, Q," Wiley said.

Sure enough, Wiley hit two out of three, and Q squealed with delight. "He did it!"

"Now ye try, Q."

Q gave it his best effort, but his face fell when he missed the target completely with all three stones.

Hoofbeats caught Maitland's attention, and he was surprised to see an unexpected trio approaching. Loki Grant tied his horse to a nearby tree and dismounted, his son Lucas and adopted son Kenzie just behind him.

Loki raised a hand in greeting to Maitland, then called out to the boys. "Let me have a look at those weapons ye are using, lads. Mayhap I have finer ones for ye."

Maitland rose to greet his friend. Though not of the same blood, anyone from Grant land felt like family to him. "Loki, so pleased to see ye, but what brings ye here?"

"We're just passing through. The lads and I always head to Ayr and Edinburgh just before Yule to search out any more lads living in crates like I did. We hope ye would oblige us with warm beds and good food for the night. We'll be moving on in the morn."

Tad came along behind the three. "The others who came with ye are already being fed. Ye are always welcome here, Loki. These are my lads, Wiley and Quillan, though we call him Q. They've been doing their best to improve their skills with their slings."

"Many thanks to ye, Tad." Loki turned to the boys and said, "Here, lads. Allow me to inspect yer slings. Mayhap Lucas has a couple spares for ye too. Not to say yers aren't good, but we're known for making the best in the land."

Wiley brought his over and said, "Greetings to ye, my lord."

Loki smiled. "Nay lord here. Just call me Loki. And this is Lucas and Kenzie. We all use slings."

Q looked up at Loki and asked, "'Ten ye hep us, peez?"

Loki ruffled Q's hair and said, "I'd love to. Will ye promise me an apple from yer orchard in return?"

"We already picked some," Wiley said. "Cook is making apple tarts for supper. Ye can have two."

"Many thanks to ye. Maitland made ye a fine sling, but try these two that Lucas has with him. He and Kenzie will teach ye the way to shoot them."

Maitland, Loki, and Tad stood back and watched

the lads practice with their new slings, cheering when they hit the target.

"Maitland, ye've been on patrol, I hear. Anything ye wish to share about yer travels?" Loki asked, crossing his arms as he watched the lads.

"Not much. The English bastards have been coming much farther north and no one likes it, but we managed to send many of them back. Or bury them."

Loki laughed. "'Tis the best place for them in the Highlands. Deep in the ground."

"Have ye seen any along yer journey?" Maitland asked.

"Nay, but we travel quickly. I only bring four others with us, so we are less than ten. And I take advantage of my friendships for shelter at night. These bones are too old to enjoy sleeping on the ground anymore. I prefer a pallet anywhere inside. I dinnae need a soft bed, just a pallet inside away from the cold of winter." He wore a thick mantle with a long scarf. "We often find a few lads and bring them home, but they are no' used to the cold Highland nights either. I am grateful for yer hospitality, Menzies."

"Think naught of it. We always enjoy seeing ye," Maitland said.

Wiley ran over to stand in front of Loki, his hand full of small stones. "Lucas gave us each a sack to carry our stones in, but he also said to always keep some to stop bad men who might be taking us away or chasing us. He said to ask ye how ye did it."

Tad chuckled along with his brother, and Loki asked, "Lucas is telling tales again, aye?"

Lucas said, "Da, 'tis a great story. Tell them how ye made the big, mean Norseman scream like a wee bairn."

Q and Wiley waited patiently, their faces full of anticipation.

"'Tis a fine secret I'll tell ye, laddies." The tall man knelt down so he was at their level.

"What is the secret?" Wiley asked.

"What secwet?" Q mimicked.

"Ye put the stones in the villain's shoes while they are sleeping. Then they canno' chase ye."

The two boys chuckled with glee and a hint of troublemaking.

"What did he do?" Wiley asked.

"What do?" Q repeated.

Loki leaned over and whispered, "A mean old Norseman I was following holed up in an abandoned house for the night. I knew I'd need to follow him when he left, but I needed to rest too. So after he went to sleep, I snuck over and put stones in his shoes. When the surly pig-nut put them on, he cursed and swore and yelled for half the hour. And I knew he was leaving so I followed him. Then I knew where he was going."

Wiley looked at Q and said, "We must fill our sacks."

The two ran off to complete their task, but Tad called out, "Ye're never to do that to yer parents or yer uncles!"

Loki laughed as the boys ran off, then his expression turned more serious. "Have ye had much problem with reivers? We haven't seen any about nor heard much news of trouble. Any insight from either of ye? We always run into marauders or reivers trying to steal sheep."

"I dinnae see any either," Maitland said. "And I agree with ye. Something is odd about that."

What the hell was going on?

THE SCOT'S RECKONING

BOOK 7

THEA AND WILLUM

The Grant and Ramsay patrol fight for the Scot's.

CHAPTER ELEVEN

The patrol runs into Loki and his lads.

WILLUM SUSPECTED THAT this patrol would be different than the others in more ways than Maitland had listed. He knew more than one member of this patrol was out for one English bastard's blood. He'd heard about the first patrol at Carlisle, when Isla and Grif had been thrown together in the dungeon, but he and Wenna had not been here then. Perhaps the next newcomers to Ramsay land would hear tales of this one.

The patrol group headed south without incident until they neared Edinburgh, when they were approached by a few members of Clan Grant.

Willum recognized Loki first, riding at the head of the small group of men. "Maitland, greetings to ye and yer patrol. Are ye interested in sharing a fine meal with us? Dobbin told me we would likely meet up with ye and chat for a bit. There's a fine clearing not far from here. We'll no' be bothered by anyone."

Dyna looked to Maitland and arched a pitiful brow at him. "If ye please? I'm famished."

Maitland nodded his agreement. "I'm hungry and would love something besides an oatcake. And 'twould be good to hear what ye have to tell us about the situation here, Loki."

Loki chuckled. "Ye are always famished, Dyna. We have plenty. I made sure to buy extra. Market day, though as ye know, when it comes to fresh food there's little available. We have plenty of dried meat and bread. We managed to find someone who still had beans, though the price was hefty."

"Wonderful," Maitland said.

Loki was traveling with his son Lucas and his grandson Dobbin. They'd brought three guards with them, as well. The two groups mixed and chatted as Loki led the way to the place they'd scouted.

They reached the clearing, and Dyna was the first off her horse. "Anyone else wish to go with me, ladies? I'm running!"

Thea laughed and hollered, "I'll join ye."

Wenna followed the two of them into the bushes, calling behind her, "Come with us, Eli. Ye canno' go alone out here."

Eli followed, and the four lasses disappeared into the woods.

The men tethered the horses, loosening saddle girths and ensuring they had enough slack in their ties to graze.

"What have ye heard about the English in Berwick Castle?" Maitland asked. "It seems Edward hasnae sent any food and the guards are now on the hunt, going in search of any animals to feed the men there."

Loki fussed with the packages tied to his saddle. "'Tis true. Sir James Douglas is still patrolling the area closest to Berwick because he's warden in the area. We happened to meet up with him before we arrived in Edinburgh. A few of the English protecting the castle sneak out occasionally in a sad attempt to find food, but he's no' seen any return. He's guessing they die from starvation or fever or are caught in the act. Meeting Douglas was a boon to our trip—we've been more alert for any news we can take back to Grant Castle. Our only intent was to shop for my daughter. Ami wanted new fabric for clothing so here we are."

Dobbin drawled, "Ami always gets what she wants. New boots too."

Lucas asked, "What are ye wearing on yer feet, Dobbin?"

"But I really needed them. She has two pairs."

Loki waved his grandson away and sat on a log in the clearing, a sack full of packages wrapped in twine piled in front of him.

"Ye have enough to share? There are eight of us, Loki. Though my belly feels like it has room for food for two." Maitland chuckled.

"Sympathy for yer wife's bigger belly?"

"Aye. True. I admit I'm excited about the prospect of our laddie."

"Ye sure 'twill be a lad?"

"Aye, we both feel it."

"Here's our largest loaf of bread. Share it amongst ye and I'll pass the sack full of apples around. They are no' the freshest, but I was surprised to find any. Someone had them in cold storage since autumn. Then I have some chicken legs that were smoked not long ago."

Willum sat down next to Maitland, Alaric next to

him. "Chicken legs. Yum. Anything but rabbit makes me happy."

As they shared the food around, the lasses returned and Dobbin started a fire for them all to gather around.

Maitland tossed the bare bone of a chicken leg into the fire. "King Robert wishes for us to keep the English in the Borderlands and trapped in Berwick until he takes the castle back. Where are we needed most? Have ye heard?"

"A group of soldiers in disguise headed into Edinburgh, begging for food so I'm told. Douglas said to find them and send them out. We couldnae locate them. Ye can try. They say they are split into two groups of five. They are stealing anything they can: food, coin, livestock. Anything they can sell or eat. And I'm told they are gaunt. They are hungry and desperate. I wish ye luck. I suggest ye search the outskirts of the city and check the taverns at night. Ye might catch them. If ye do, bring them to Douglas. He'll handle them."

Willum had to admit the thought of this tactic made his skin crawl. He didn't wish to go inside any tavern, since they were often filled with unwashed men wall-to-wall. That was exactly the type of situation that could make him lose his head.

Crowds in tight spaces.

Being alone in the woods.

His two biggest fears. With eight of them, he needn't worry about being alone, especially with Maitland's rules about always traveling in pairs.

But he didn't like the idea of Edinburgh. Any burgh made his insides curdle from distaste.

Loki and his group took their leave after the meal, heading back into the Highlands.

"Dyna, let's no' waste any time," Maitland said. "If we're looking for English thieves in Edinburgh, then we should find a place to sleep this eve. We'll split up. Choose yer team and we'll get on our way."

"I'll take Thea, Alaric, and Willum. Work for ye?"

"Aye, off to Edinburgh. There are two inns I know where the questionable oft shelter. I'll take the worst of the two places. Ye take the other."

Willum let out a breath. He was more than pleased to have Thea with him.

Perhaps he'd get the chance to steal a kiss. A real one.

AYRSHIRE-SURVIVAL 1263

A new scene for you showing both Lucky Loki and Wise Loki.

Tissue warning. Have them ready…

LOKI WOKE UP with a sneeze, hitting his head on the top of the weathered crate. Hell, but it had rained half the night and he was soaked. He needed a tarp to cover the crate, though he would soon outgrow the meager shelter. He had to find something to keep him dry overnight through the damp spring.

He blew his nose on his hand and wiped it off on a nearby stone, hating his life. At times like these, he would spend half the day trying to recall anything about his parents.

Why had they given him away?

Had he done something to make them hate him? Father Adair had told him some families had too many children to feed so they gave their bairns away or even sold them. Was he just pushed out the door, or had they traded him for something? But the priest had also reminded him that his parents could have simply passed on from illness.

Every night when he went to bed, he said a wee prayer for God to let him dream something about his parents or his family.

He had to know. It was an ache deep inside him that would not be eased. That hollow place in his chest was worse than the emptiness of his belly.

After taking care of his few belongings—the pot, his extra tunic and trews that were too small but he kept anyway, and the few linen squares he'd stolen to wash his face and hands when they were covered with dirt—he got to his feet and stretched. He leaned against the tree he kept his crate under for extra shelter from both the elements and some of the unsavory characters in the area. Sadly, his belly no longer grumbled. It was too used to being empty.

It hadn't been a good week. He'd had little too eat, hadn't been able to find any coin, and Father Adair, his only friend, had gone on a journey of some sort. He could usually count on obtaining an apple from the priest, but not this day.

He groaned and pushed off from the tree, the rain letting up enough for him to head to town. This day he had purpose.

He would search for a tarp or length of thick canvas to keep his sad home dry.

And a piece of bread.

Mayhap he'd beg a stale loaf from the local bakery, though they usually only threw crumbs at him to make him leave. One baker was kind and would feed him a hardened crust on occasion, but only what they couldn't sell.

Selfish pignuts.

As he entered the center of town, his gaze searched the area to make sure the evil bastards who liked to tease him were not about. He stopped when he caught sight of something more important.

Behind one of the market stalls, a large piece of tarp had been set across a row of bushes to dry now that the rain had ended.

Loki needed that tarp. He took a few steps toward the stall, but the owner appeared so he walked away, vowing to keep checking on the prized fabric.

He trudged down the way and into the center of the burgh where more market stalls began to open up. He could feel a rumbling against his foot through the hole in his boot as he walked; soon a sound rose up to match the vibrations. It sounded like thunder, and he could see everyone else around the market felt the same. They all wandered about looking puzzled until the source of the din appeared. If it were a usual day, the cloud of dust would have been visible first.

But this was not a usual day in the burgh of Ayr.

A group of riders on the biggest horses Loki had ever seen raced down the main road toward the castle. He gaped at the spectacle of warriors dressed in red and green plaids galloping through Ayr. Each man had a massive sword strapped to his saddle or his back, sheaths and hilts gleaming in the sun just breaking through the clouds. He ran over to get a closer look.

Who were they?

He listened as two vendors began to discuss the sight.

"King Alexander said a couple of the clans from the deep Highlands would be coming to his aid. Haakon said he's attacking with a fleet of galley ships."

"How many ships?"

"I heard two score."

Another man called out. "I heard four score. That's why the savage Highlanders are here. Let's hope they protect us."

The man closest to him said, "Those warriors are from Clan Grant. Everyone knows the red plaids. They're the strongest clan in all the Highlands. I'm glad they're here."

Loki took three steps closer until he could look the warriors in the eye. That was what he wanted—

to be so bold and brave and to have a whole clan around him. What would it take to be a Grant warrior? He wished to be on one of those giant destriers, riding a majestic beast for all to see, his arms the size of tree trunks. One warrior smiled at him and tossed him something. He caught it, surprised to see it was an oatcake. He was so hungry that he nearly swallowed it whole before he recalled his manners, choked the food down, and called out, "My thanks to ye."

There were more horses than he'd ever seen. Once they were gone, he moved closer to the three men chatting.

"How far did they come?" He had to know, because that was his new goal in life, to make his way to Grant land to become a warrior.

A savage Highlander.

"Half a day's fast ride, at least. Probable nearly a day, lad. You cannot walk there. You'd never make it through the mountains."

"Are the mountains big?"

"They're a sight to see, for certe. I hope you get to see it someday."

Loki nodded and moved on, knowing the merchant would only laugh if Loki told him how determined he was to get there. He made his way over toward the stall where he'd seen the tarp, disappointed to see it was gone.

A few moments later, he heard something stirring behind him and whirled around to face the same canvas being tossed over his head. Someone shoved him, tripping him into the material, and they wrapped him in the smelly wet fabric and tossed him into the air a few times, then tossed him into a tree trunk. Loki's neck snapped back, slamming his head into the solid wood.

Stunned, he didn't move after he landed, but his laughing tormenters unwrapped him, whipping the canvas away.

"You should pay attention, Loki."

"Bugger off, ye surly arsewipes."

"Arsewipe, am I?" The tallest one reached over and swung his arm out, catching the side of Loki's head and snapping it sideways. "I'd keep your words inside or I'll beat them back into you, wise arse."

The second one guffawed. "Aye, fool. We saw ye drooling after those warriors like you thought you might have a prayer of joining them. Do you think the Grants would ever accept you?"

"They'd never let you step inside their curtain wall, you're so dirty."

"You stink, you're dirty, and you're naught but a useless bag of bones."

"And you're ugly too."

The three boys, a few years older than him and much bigger, strode away laughing.

Someday he'd show them. Loki swore it on his mother's unknown name.

THE PARAPETS, MANY YEARS LATER.

Castle Curanta, winter, 1319

Loki Grant sat on a stool on the parapets. While the biting wind made his eyes water, the glistening there was from more than the wind. His face fell into his hands and he set his elbows on his knees and allowed the tears to fall freely.

The door opened and one of his cherished grandsons, Ketill, stuck his head around the corner. "Grandda, Da is looking for you."

Loki lifted his head and let out a long breath between his pursed lips. "Tell your da I'll be down in a bit."

"'Tis cold up here, Grandda."

"It is, but I'm fine." He turned to gaze at the young lad of seven years, about the age he'd been when Brodie Grant had found him hiding behind a tree in Ayr.

"Grandda, are you crying? Why?" Ketill moved over and set his hands on his grandsire's knee and leaned in closer to take a good look at the tears dampening his cheeks.

"'Tis from the wind, Ketill."

Ketill studied him a wee bit longer, then said, "Nay, I think they're true tears. Is it because of Great-Grandda Brodie?"

Loki wasn't about to lie to the lad. He knew the truth of all that had happened. The messenger had arrived two nights ago to tell them that his father, Brodie Grant, had passed away in his sleep at Muir Castle, leaving his dear mother, Celestina, heartbroken.

He nodded and said, "Aye. I miss him already."

Ketill, sticking to the important facts of life as he knew them, said, "He was nearly ninety winters old. Do you not think that is old? He's the only one that old, is he not?"

"Aye. Uncle Robbie and Aunt Caralyn, Uncle

Alex and Aunt Maddie have all passed on. Aunt Brenna is a few years younger. Aunt Jennie is much younger. She's still in her seventh decade. And then there's Uncle Logan." He had to think about that one for a bit. How old was the old warrior? He had to be close to ninety.

"How old is he?"

"I don't think anyone truly knows."

Ketill looked over his shoulder and whispered, "I dinnae think Uncle Logan will ever die. Do you?"

Loki chuckled and said, "Someday he will." He reached for the lad and settled him on his lap, hoping to warm him, but these days, the young ones warmed him.

Ketill scowled and stared at him. "So why do you cry so?"

"Lad, my memories are haunting me. The mind does odd things sometimes."

Ketill stared up at his beloved grandsire. "Good memories or bad ones?"

Loki chuckled, the child wiser than he ever was. "Both."

The lad scrunched his face up the way he did when he had to think hard. "From the time you lived in the crate? How *did* you live in a crate? I would not know how to do that. It would be cold, would it not?"

"Cold and hard and hungry. That's what it's like living in a crate. Do you have time for a wee tale or two, lad?"

Ketill nodded, grabbing the fur across Loki's lap and moving it over his legs, snuggling underneath.

"I love your tales, Grandda. Especially the ones about the battles."

"This is not quite about a battle. This is about an evil man. Shall I?"

"Aye, do tell."

"When I was your age and I lived in the crate, every day I did the same things. I would run to the taverns to try to beg for scraps, then to a bakery to ask for a stale loaf of bread, then I would go to the center of town to see what was transpiring near the king's castle. After that, I would go check on a lass I called Missy Angel."

"Great-Grandmama?"

"Aye. She was the loveliest in all the land, but she had the saddest eyes I'd ever seen."

"How could you see her that close?"

"I would look every morning to see her pull the fur back on her window and stick her head out to take deep breaths. Sometimes I saw her cry. Once I saw someone grab her arm and yank her back inside the tower."

"Who?"

"A man known as the Baron."

"He was evil? He must have been if he treated a lass like that."

"Aye. Let me tell you about this one particular day. It had rained that night, and I'd gone to the market, hoping to steal a tarp."

"But stealing is wrong."

Loki chuckled, pleased to hear that Lucas had taught him well. "I know, but I didn't know so back then, nor had I any coin to buy what I needed. Now, listen to the tale."

"I'm listening." The lad's eyes locked on his, waiting for the tale to continue.

"So that day at the market, I'd seen a group of warriors go by, and I learned they were Grant warriors. How I wished to be one of them! When the warriors had ridden off, the mean boys of the burgh ambushed me, wrapped me up in a tarp, and tossed me about before throwing me against a tree."

Ketill leaped off Loki's lap and began to swing his fists. "I'd punch them for you, Grandda. Like this." Then he swung his fists and kicked a leg up.

"And I would appreciate that, but they were bigger than you and me. And I was outnumbered. But what they didn't realize is they did me a favor."

"What favor?"

"They were so mean and I was so tired of their bullying that I wanted more than ever to be a Grant warrior."

Ketill settled back on his lap sideways so he could watch him.

"Once I was able to get away, I ran to look for Missy Angel. But that particular day, she didn't appear. I waited and waited, but I never saw her, so I walked around the entire castle to see if she'd gone to a new chamber. I waited a while, then circled again, looking for her. Sometimes she was late peeking out, but I had nowhere to go, so I waited. All was quiet. Then I heard her. She was at a side window trying to climb out. I yelled at her to stop because she'd fall, but she didn't hear me."

"How could she not hear you?"

"Because of all the ruckus the warhorses were making coming down the path. I turned around and saw the biggest black horse I'd ever seen coming straight for me, a score of horses behind him. I hid in the bushes as they approached, but one warrior stopped his mount because of the angel. He'd seen her trying to climb out."

"Which one was Great-Grandda?"

"The one who stopped. Uncle Alex, on the black destrier, yelled at him to keep moving, but he refused. When the angel saw him, she dropped the furs and fell back inside. Your Great Grandda went up to the door and banged on it, but they wouldn't let him in. I could see how upset he was and how angry he was with the man at the door. But he left and went on his way. That's when I got my idea."

"What idea?"

"How I could get some coin from the man who was so interested in Missy Angel. I returned to the burgh and found out that they were also Clan Grant warriors. It turned out this group was the Grant laird and his best warriors—fiercer and stronger than the first force I'd seen. And I found out over the next couple of days that one man kept sneaking into her manor, so I knew I could get coin from him."

"How? Why would he give you a coin?"

There was that scrunched up face he loved again. Ketill was a joy to watch. But Loki forced himself to continue. "Because I knew he was searching for Missy Angel, and I knew her better than he did."

"Did he give you a coin?"

"He did, but it took a while. One day, I was listening to him talk with his friend in the burgh and he caught me, threatened to get me in trouble until I told him what I knew about Missy Angel."

"Then he liked you, because she's Great-Grandmama. And you helped him find her."

"Aye."

"So what was the best part of the tale? I know you saved Grandmama and brought her to Grant land. And you got Grandda home after his leg was cut."

"The best part. Hmmm. Two things stand out in my mind."

"Tell me both!"

"The first one was the first meat pie that Da bought me—he wasn't my da yet, of course. It was lamb and so juicy that it ran down my chin. I swear it was the best meat pie I've ever eaten."

"Better than scraps?"

"Much better than scraps."

"What are scraps?"

"Scraps? Mostly stale bread, moldy vegetables, and rows of fat cut from meat that people wouldn't eat."

"Och. I would not like that. What was the second one? Did the mean boys come after you and you punched them?"

Loki's head fell back, a swift memory had popped into his head. "Lad, I forgot about that. My thanks for asking because now I recall. When Brodie put me up on his horse once, I looked over at the leader of the mean boys who harassed me. He'd appeared out of nowhere with his fist in the air."

"He saw you with Great-Grandda?"

"He did." How had he forgotten this part? The fool had cursed at him from a distance.

"What did you do?"

"I waved at him, grinning."

Ketill giggled, his hand over his mouth. "I wish I'd

been there for that. So that was your other favorite memory?"

"Nay. My favorite memory of all time was the moment Uncle Alex told me that Great-Grandda and Great-Grandmama wanted to adopt me. I didn't think anyone would ever want me."

"Why not? I love you, Grandda."

"Back then, I thought my mama and da gave me away. If my own parents didn't want me, I thought I must be unlovable. I learned the story wasn't true later on, as a child, I believed the worst. And when they agreed to adopt me, I knew I had a home."

The door opened and his son Lucas emerged. "Da, why don't you come down. It's cold up here."

Loki ruffled Ketill's hair. "I'm on my way. Ketill was keeping me company, but the wind is getting stronger. Inside with you, laddie." He followed his son and grandson down the stairs, stopping at his chamber.

Lucas paused with him and said, "Da, I'll go with you to Muir Castle. I'm sure you'd like to see your mama."

"Nay, she has Catriona and Alison and Braden and a slew of grandbairns to watch over her. I'd probably just get in the way." He didn't know how to explain that being an orphan had a way of making you feel as if you belonged on the outside. His parents had always made him feel loved, but he knew how others thought.

He stepped inside his chamber and grabbed another plaid to wrap around himself. He was still chilled from the wind. Lucas and Ketill went below stairs while he did his best to untangle his long strands of hair from the wind's effect. He moved over to warm himself by the embers in the hearth.

A wee bit later, a voice rang out. "Grandda!"

"Coming," he said, knowing they'd all wish to comfort him after losing his father. The man who'd meant everything to him, who'd taught him what love and fairness and pride and honesty and diligence meant. He'd miss him terribly. Even though he hadn't seen him often in the past few years, he'd stopped at least a few times a year to visit with him.

To listen to his wisdom and to see the undying love in his gaze. After all these years, the man still loved him.

Not nearly as much as Loki loved Brodie and Celestina Grant.

"Loki Grant, get out here right now."

His eyes widened and he turned, then froze. That voice sounded just like his mother. He had to be imagining things. Taking slow steps out to the balcony, he finally gained the courage to peek over the railing, surprised to see his beloved mother standing there, Braden and Cairstine right behind her.

"Mama? What are you doing here? You should be home in mourning."

The lovely woman with the long white hair flowing down her back held something out to him. "I'm doing what your father asked me to do. Come down here, if you please."

He made his way down the stairs, his gaze traveling across all the faces in the crowd from Muir Castle, his sisters and brother and their families. He stepped in front of his mother and bussed her cheek.

"Mama, I'm so sorry." And the tears flowed down his cheeks again before he could finish his thoughts.

His mother reached up to cup his cheek. "I've accepted it. We lived a beautiful life together, blessed with bairns and grandbairns, and that never would have happened without your help. Your da wanted you to have this." She held out a long, cloth-wrapped bundle. He took it and settled it on a nearby table, unwrapping it carefully, shocked to see what sat inside.

"Mama, you must have made a mistake."

There, inside the wrapping, sat a sheathed sword. Loki recognized it instantly. It was the one Brodie had used in the Battle of Largs. The sword he used against Ivarsson, the cruel bastard, Brodie Grant's most prized possession. It hung on the wall over the hearth at Muir Castle for many years.

"This belongs with Braden." He picked it up, savoring the feel of the worn grip in his hands, his gaze traveling over the two gemstones embedded in the pommel, and the sharpened edge that had helped secure Scotland's safety from the Norse.

His mother set her hand on his. "Nay, Loki. He wanted you to have it. It's only because of you that Brodie found me so many times, because of you that he made it to the healer after he was injured at Largs. We adore Braden, but you are our first son, and you deserve it. He asked me to bring this to you."

He looked to his brother, but Braden nodded in

agreement. "You fought with him at Largs when he used that sword, Loki. You deserve it."

Stunned, he had no words. He hugged his mother, then moved over to the wall displaying his family's weapons and took down his old sword. With a deep breath, he set his sire's sword in its place. It was the best spot on the wall. Turning back, he opened his arm to his mother and tucked her up next to him, Bella on the other side, and they admired it together.

"I'll miss you, Da, but I'll never forget all you taught me."

Highland Highlights
The Best of...

Alexander Grant, Part 1 and 2
Madeline Grant
Brenna Grant
Logan Ramsay, Part 1 and 2
Gwyneth Ramsay
Loki Grant
Torrian Ramsay
Connor Grant
Maitland Menzie
Dyna Grant
The Bairns, Part 1 and 2
The Pets, The Ghosts, and Spirits
My Favorite Scenes

ABOUT THE AUTHOR

KEIRA MONTCLAIR IS the pen name of an author who lives in South Carolina with her husband. She loves to write fast-paced, emotional romance, especially with children as secondary characters.

When she's not writing, she loves to spend time with her grandchildren. She's worked as a high school math teacher, a registered nurse, and an office manager. She loves ballet, mathematics, puzzles, learning anything new, and creating new characters for her readers to fall in love with.

She writes historical romantic suspense. Her best-selling series is a family saga that follows two medieval Scottish clans through four generations and now numbers over fifty books.

Contact her through her website:
www.keiramontclair.com

www.ingramcontent.com/pod-product-compliance
Lightning Source LLC
LaVergne TN
LVHW010654110826
845149LV00014B/3087

* 9 7 8 1 9 7 2 6 0 1 0 7 5 *